To — Addi.
for your "half"
Birthday
love +
Grandmama

4-1-13

Missing:
Mrs. Cornblossom

Missing:
Mrs. Cornblossom

COLLEEN ANDERSON

QUARRIER PRESS
CHARLESTON, WV

Quarrier Press
Charleston, WV

Layout and cover design by Colleen Anderson

This book is a work of fiction. Any similarities
to real people, living or dead, are purely
coincidental. All characters and events in this
work are products of the author's imagination.

Library of Congress Control Number: 2012940158

10 9 8 7 6 5 4 3 2 1

ISBN-13: 978-1-891852-84-8
ISBN-10: 1-891852-84-1

Distributed by West Virginia Book Company

www.wvbookco.com

In memory of Wil and Edna Morse

CHAPTER ONE:
MRS. CORNBLOSSOM DISAPPEARS

Day came to Arlington Court as it always had. The sky brightened. Light seeped through the east windows. Inside the courtyard, however, shadows lingered between the two rows of houses, dim and mysterious.

From a windowsill two stories above, the cat Cocobean peered through the glass. She was a comely cat, compact and calico, and she looked very pretty sitting there, although no one was watching.

Cocobean spied a lone light shining in the front window of old Mrs. Cornblossom's house. What could it mean? Why was Mrs. Cornblossom awake so early?

The cat jumped from the sill with a light thump. The sound did not wake her master, Toothbucket. He continued to snore softly, dreaming of coffee and cream, French toast and jam.

Cocobean took a seat on the floor a few inches from Toothbucket's nose, and stared. "Wake up," she thought. He didn't wake. She leaped to the bed and walked on top of his quilt-covered body, up and down the length of his sleeping form. She purred in his ear. Still he didn't move. She tickled his neck, just underneath his beard, with her whiskers. At this, Toothbucket stirred, rolled over, and mumbled, "Mmmpphh. Sleeping."

Cocobean vaulted from the bed. She ran from the room and down the empty staircase, heading straight for the little cat door Toothbucket had built into the bottom of his front door. Darting through the cat door, she left two perfect paw prints on a piece of paper that lay in her path.

Outward she went, into the day not quite begun, into the night not quite gone. Into the place that was her home, and Toothbucket's home, and indeed, the home of everyone she knew and loved, and everything that made up her world: Arlington Court.

Holding her tail high in the air and twitching its tip as she went, Cocobean turned onto the main sidewalk and sauntered along. The sidewalk in the center of the court ran the whole length, from one end to the other. At each end was an iron gate with a latch.

The cat stopped to listen. No birds sang. No crickets chirped. Even beyond the gates of Arlington Court, all was quiet. The city was still asleep. No dogs barked. No horns wailed. How peaceful it was!

But now a small sound came to Cocobean's attention—a muffled, snuffly noise. And she heard words: "Will they miss me when I am gone? I have lived many places in my life, but this was the best."

The speaker was Mrs. Cornblossom. She sat alone in the wooden swing on her front porch, yet she spoke as if someone were beside her. But there was no one, only a suitcase on the top step. Mrs. Cornblossom was crying.

Cocobean turned up the walk to Mrs. Cornblossom's house and bounced up the steps to the old woman's side. When she saw the cat, Mrs. Cornblossom dried her tears on her apron and said, "Cocobean, good morning. You have caught an old woman feeling sorry for herself." She stroked the cat's chin, who nuzzled one of the old woman's nubby socks in appreciation.

"You see, I am going to die," Mrs. Cornblossom told Cocobean. "And I don't mind that so much, for I have lived a long and happy life. Just the same, I will miss this place. I will miss the children. And Toothbucket, dear old Toothbucket, I will miss him most of all."

Holding onto the doorknob for support, Mrs. Cornblossom pulled herself to her feet and looked over the rail of her porch. She surveyed the garden. In the grey-blue light, it seemed larger than it was. Everything fit together so well and every plant was so healthy that the garden seemed perfect, like a jewel. The squash plants did not ramble, but stayed in their places. They sprouted fountains of foliage—huge, stiff leaves that hid gold blossoms and zucchinis as big as Cocobean. Green, red, and yellow bell peppers dangled like holiday ornaments from their bushes. Morning glory vines twined up strings along the porch and bloomed at regular intervals, like musicians on parade. Already they were unfurling their petal trumpets. A patch of tasselled corn grew next to a stand of tall canna lilies whose tops blazed like torches. Closer to the ground, all around the vegetables, nestled small flowers. And at the far end of Mrs. Cornblossom's garden, where it adjoined Toothbucket's garden, was a handsome pawpaw tree with deep green, drooping leaves.

"I will miss my garden, too," Mrs. Cornblossom sighed. "I wonder if there will be a garden where I am going."

Then, as if she had heard something even a cat could not hear, old Mrs. Cornblossom sighed and shuffled into her house. When she came out again a few minutes later, her apron was gone and her stockings were laced into sturdy brown shoes. With one last look at the garden, she picked up her suitcase and hobbled down the steps. She made her way along the sidewalk. Cautiously, Cocobean followed. When Mrs. Cornblossom came to the end of the sidewalk, she set down the suitcase to unlatch the gate. Then she latched it again behind her.

"Goodbye, Cocobean," she said. "You must go home now. And I must leave Arlington Court. I have one more journey to make."

Cocobean watched Mrs. Cornblossom go to the corner, limping slightly. She watched the old woman turn the corner and disappear from sight. Then Cocobean padded softly back to Toothbucket's house and entered through the cat door.

CHAPTER TWO:
TOOTHBUCKET'S NEW NEIGHBOR

Toothbucket liked to wake up slowly, one part of him at a time. After he was aware of being himself, but before he opened his eyes, he lay quietly and waited for the last shreds of dream to float away like river mist. He stretched each of his long limbs in turn—right arm, right leg, left leg, left arm. Sometimes he went the other way around, beginning with the left arm and ending with the right arm. Next, he stretched them all at once while uttering his first sound of the day, a lengthy and satisfying yawn. He gave his beard a bracing tug. Then, and only then, Toothbucket opened his eyes.

The cat Cocobean sat beside the bed with her tail curled in front of her, watching him. Toothbucket reached out a big hand and stroked her head, bending back her ears. Cocobean made a trill of pleasure.

"Good morning, little Cocobean," said Toothbucket. "Yes, it's time to get out of bed, isn't it?" He pulled one foot from under the quilt and set it on the floor. The other foot followed. He sat for a moment on the edge of the bed, with his hands on his knees, as if he had forgotten what came next. Then, with a sound that was half a sigh and half a grunt, Toothbucket stood.

He was very tall and quite thin. Even his fingers and toes were long and thin, and his bones bulged at every joint—elbow, knee, and knuckle.

Toothbucket put on his overalls, went downstairs, and turned toward the kitchen. A scrap of white caught his attention; a piece of paper was lodged under the cat door he had made for Cocobean. He bent to pick it up. It was an envelope. On the outside were several paw prints. Inside was a letter.

"Dear Toothbucket," the letter began, "by the time you read this, I shall be gone. Please forgive me for stealing away in this cowardly manner. I will miss you so much, my dear old Toothbucket."

She had signed the letter, "Your true friend, Edna Cornblossom."

There was one more line, an afterthought in Mrs. Cornblossom's shaky hand: "Toothbucket, will you look after my garden?"

Toothbucket opened his front door and stepped out onto the porch. He looked across the garden to his neighbor's porch. Her swing swayed slightly in the morning breeze, as if an invisible Mrs. Cornblossom sat there, rocking gently. He couldn't believe she was gone.

Toothbucket was used to helping Mrs. Cornblossom in the garden. At the beginning of each winter, he heaped dry leaves on the flowerbeds to keep them cozy. He covered the roots of Mrs. Cornblossom's beloved pawpaw tree with a pile of leaves. When spring came, Toothbucket smoothed the leaves and waited for the garden to come alive. He watched Mrs. Cornblossom's crocuses and daffodils and trilliums poke their heads out of the earth. He saw the first blossoms on the pawpaw tree—small brown buttons that opened into bells, like tiny doll dresses hanging from the branches.

Every summer, when plump fruits hung in place of the purple blossoms, Toothbucket and Mrs. Cornblossom worked together in the garden, pulling weeds. Together they watched as morning glories climbed the strings, peppers popped out, and tomatoes grew fat.

Toothbucket carried the letter inside. In the kitchen, Cocobean sat on the floor, staring intently at her empty food bowl. Toothbucket opened a can of tuna fish and spooned some into the bowl. Cocobean walked all around it, inspecting her breakfast. Finally she took one dainty bite.

As for Toothbucket, he had lost his appetite.

Cocobean took another bite of tuna fish. Suddenly, she cocked her head and listened. Toothbucket listened, too. He heard voices.

With the cat bounding ahead, he went out to see what was happening.

From the porch, Toothbucket and Cocobean saw two sturdy men open the gate and come up the walk. They carried a tall grandfather clock, one man holding each end. They took the clock up the steps to Mrs. Cornblossom's porch and set it down gently.

Toothbucket cleared his throat. "This is Mrs. Cornblossom's house," he said. "Are you sure you have the right address?"

One of the men took a piece of paper from his pocket and looked at it. "Yes," he said, "this is the right address. Mrs. Cornbosom has sold her house."

"Corn-Blossom!" Toothbucket corrected the man sharply.

The workman shrugged and said, "Whatever." And the two men went back down the walk.

Toothbucket sat down in his old, creaky rocking chair. Cocobean jumped into his lap. "Mrs. Cornblossom is gone," Toothbucket told Cocobean. Then he began to cry.

Before long, however, Toothbucket stopped crying and started to think. "I wonder who is coming to live in

Mrs. Cornblossom's house," he said to himself. "I wonder if the new neighbor will like me."

For the rest of the morning, Toothbucket sat on his front porch to watch the goings-on at Mrs. Cornblossom's house. Workers carried furniture into the house—a brass bed, a tall cupboard with glass doors, a desk, a large table, four chairs with needlepoint roses on their seats, two lamps, and more clocks. In fact, there were more clocks than Toothbucket could count. Grandfather clocks! Grandmother clocks! Cuckoo clocks! Small clocks, medium-sized clocks, and clocks even taller than Toothbucket.

Toothbucket didn't own a single clock. He woke up with the sun and went to bed with the moon. He ate when he was hungry and fed Cocobean when she stared at her dish.

What happened next happened very slowly, for that is the way Toothbucket did everything. Slowly, a smile spread across his face. Slowly, his eyes began to shine. He stretched his lanky form and got up from his chair. He had a good idea.

He went into the garden. There, hiding near the bottom of a large tomato plant, he found a perfectly ripe tomato, as big as his fist. He carried it inside. From the refrigerator, he took a jar of mayonnaise. From the breadbox, he took two slices of fresh bread. He made a tomato sandwich. He cut the sandwich into four triangles and arranged them on his very best plate, the blue one without any chips or cracks.

Suddenly, a calico shape flashed under his nose. The cat Cocobean leaped to the kitchen counter, snatched a triangle of sandwich, and fled, knocking the plate to the floor with a clatter. It broke into three pieces. The rest of the sandwich lay on the floor.

Toothbucket's floor, sad to say, was not very clean.

"Oh, Cocobean, you naughty cat!" he cried. "That sandwich was a gift for our new neighbor! And now my best plate is broken!" With a sigh, he picked up his gift from the floor. He put the three remaining triangles of sandwich into Cocobean's bowl. He dropped the broken china into his wastebasket. Now, how would he welcome the stranger?

Toothbucket felt very tired. He trudged outside to his rocking chair. He was getting ready to cry again when he saw a most unusual sight.

A very short person came up the walk, staggering under the weight of yet another large clock. He teetered this way and that, nearly dropping his burden at every step. He was as broad as he was tall, yet he wore a handsome three-piece suit that fit him just exactly, and a straw hat with a red feather in the hatband.

The little man had reached the door of Mrs. Cornblossom's house. He lowered the clock to the porch. From the pocket of his vest, he pulled a white kerchief. He unfolded it carefully. He took off his hat. Toothbucket gasped. The man had no hair, not so much as a tuft of hair anywhere on his head. He was bald as an egg.

The short man wiped his shiny head with the kerchief and replaced his hat at a jaunty angle. Then he pulled a pocket watch—yes, another clock!—from his other vest pocket. He looked at it, nodded, and put it back into the pocket. He went into Mrs. Cornblossom's house.

Toothbucket waited for nearly an hour, but the little man didn't come out again.

Toothbucket rocked and thought. The more he thought, the sadder he became. Finally, he made a decision. He would go over to Mrs. Cornblossom's house and say hello. He would try to be friendly. His heart wasn't in it, but what else could he do?

He made his way through the garden toward Mrs. Cornblossom's house. As unhappy as he was, Toothbucket couldn't help but notice the beautiful garden. The August lilies waved like small flags on their stems, sending out a delicious smell. Or perhaps the fragrance came from the autumn-flowering clematis, frothy as sea foam, that crawled along the picket fence in front of Mrs. Cornblossom's house. No, it was neither of these. The smell was sweeter. It reminded him of something.

Toothbucket looked down. At his feet, so close that he would have flattened it with his next step, lay a ripe pawpaw—the first of the season. He bent to pick it up. It was green with brown specks and soft to the touch. It was about the size of a small potato. He could almost taste the sweet custard of his favorite fruit.

If Mrs. Cornblossom had been there, he would have brought her the fruit. She would have squealed with anticipation and gone to fetch two spoons. They would have sat on her porch swing, scooping out the yellow flesh, exclaiming over each bite, tasting the sweetness of early autumn.

Now, what would happen? What if the new neighbor didn't like the pawpaw tree? What if he cut it down?

With a heavy heart, Toothbucket climbed the four steps to Mrs. Cornblossom's house. He rang the bell. He waited.

The door flew open. Standing there was the fat little man, without his hat. Toothbucket looked down at the shiny top of his head. Then, in a voice shaking with fear, he said, "I am Toothbucket, your neighbor. Welcome." He held out the pawpaw.

The little man tipped his head back and looked into Toothbucket's face. He took the pawpaw from Toothbucket and looked at it. Then he sniffed it.

"Is it something to eat?" he said at last.

"Yes, it's a pawpaw," said Toothbucket. "Mrs. Cornblossom loved pawpaws. It grew on our tree." He pointed to the tree.

"Excellent!" cried the man. "Do come in! It's nearly teatime, and I haven't a thing to offer you but tea. No scones, no clotted cream, no jam! I'm terribly embarrassed! How very kind of you! Come in, come in! Toothbucket, you say? Inchbald's my name. Delighted to make your acquaintance!"

He ushered Toothbucket into the house, chattering all the while. Cocobean, not to be left out, scooted between their legs.

Toothbucket looked around in astonishment. In the front room, the table was laid with a china plate and a teacup on a saucer, a silver spoon, a linen napkin, and a teapot covered with a quilted tea-cozy. Around the table were the chairs, each seat embroidered with needlepoint roses. In one corner was the cupboard with glass doors, already filled with plates, bowls, cups, and saucers. On every wall and every mantel were clocks. The air was filled with contented ticking sounds.

Inchbald bustled about. He brought another cup, saucer, plate, and silver spoon. From a drawer below the cupboard, he took another napkin.

"There we have it!" he exclaimed. "Please sit down! Now, about this fruit, this...pawpaw. Whatever shall we do with it?"

Carefully, Toothbucket broke the pawpaw into two pieces. He put one piece on Inchbald's plate. The yellow flesh glistened. He put the other piece on his own plate. With one of the silver spoons, he scooped out a bite of pawpaw custard. He held it out to Inchbald. "Taste," he said.

Inchbald took the spoon and tasted. Toothbucket

held his breath. Inchbald's eyes grew round, and his whole face smiled. He swallowed.

"Exquisite!" cried Inchbald. "Positively wonderful! I love it!" Inchbald poured tea into two cups. He lifted one. "Cheers!" he sang out.

Toothbucket's heart seemed to grow in his chest. As much as he missed Mrs. Cornblossom, he was going to like the new neighbor. Even better, the new neighbor was going to like him.

"Inchbald," he said, "I think we are going to get on well."

"Of course we are," Inchbald agreed. Then, suddenly, he pulled his pocket watch from his vest and consulted it. He held a finger to his lips. "Hush," he said, "listen!"

From every corner of the house, clocks began to sound the hour. Some made deep gonging sounds. Others played chiming tunes. A cuckoo bird flew out of a tiny door and called, "Cuckoo! Cuckoo! Cuckoo! Cuckoo!" Mrs. Cornblossom's old house was filled with bells and music.

In the corner, Cocobean jumped straight into the air and landed on all four paws, frozen.

As suddenly as they had started, the clocks went back to their soft ticking. The cuckoo backed into its birdhouse.

Toothbucket's mouth hung open. Finally he said, "That was lovely."

"Indeed it was," said Inchbald. "And it's only four o'clock now. Just wait until you hear it at twelve o'clock. It's exactly three times better."

CHAPTER THREE:
GINGERBREAD EMERGENCY

It was a glorious fall day. Sunlight poured from a cloudless sky like honey from a deep, blue bowl. Orange and yellow leaves drifted from maple trees and settled on the sidewalk that ran the length of Arlington Court. Two monarch butterflies, who resembled falling leaves themselves, floated and fluttered among them. In the garden, a drowsy bee hovered over a clump of wine-colored chrysanthemums. The cat Cocobean dozed in a puddle of sunlight on the third step leading to Inchbald's front door.

The door was open. From within came music—not the chiming of clocks that echoed through the house every hour, but the sounds of an orchestra and a choir. A man's booming voice sang alone for a time. Soon a chorus of other voices joined it. Horns called, and the silvery music of violins flowed like waves. The song went along with an orderly rhythm.

From time to time, the sound of Inchbald's voice, squeaky but right on key, joined the choir: "Hallelujah! Hallelujah!"

Inchbald was in his kitchen. The rotund little gentleman fairly filled the small room. He was still wearing his flop-eared, fuzzy bunny slippers and his red flannel nightshirt, which reached all the way to his chubby knees. Over the nightshirt, he had tied a white apron with a frill of ruffled eyelet at the hem. He had found the apron hanging on a hook behind the kitchen door, and guessed, correctly, that Mrs. Cornblossom had left it there. He supposed she wouldn't mind his wearing it. The strings barely reached around him, but once he got them fastened, Inchbald was very pleased with Mrs. Cornblossom's apron.

In one hand, he held a wooden spoon, waving it like a symphony conductor in time with the music that blared from the record player in the parlor.

The song swelled in a crescendo. Although there was barely room for him to turn around between the countertops, Inchbald set himself spinning in a pirouette. He raised the spoon above his head. The ruffles on Mrs. Cornblossom's apron flew up and twirled about him like a ballerina's tutu.

The music ended, but Inchbald was still whirling when he spied three small faces peering through the open doorway. He stopped and regarded three children. They were pointing at him and giggling.

"What is so amusing?" he asked them sharply.

"Oh, nothing," said the smallest of the three. "We heard singing, and then we looked and saw you dancing, and..." She failed to finish the sentence because she was taken with a new fit of giggling. Then they were at it again, all three laughing so hard that they had to hold onto one another to stay upright.

Inchbald drew himself up to his full height, which was not very high. "There is something much more important taking place here, my dears. I am not merely singing and dancing. I am cooking."

The three stopped laughing at once, and crowded closer in the doorway. Inchbald surveyed them. The one who had spoken was a small, pert, dark-haired girl with a rosy complexion. Her friends, who might have been a year or two older, were taller—one a thin, pale youth with thick glasses and a thoughtful face, and the other a sturdy, handsome lad with a dimpled chin.

"What are you cooking?" said the talkative one. "Something good?"

"Why would anyone go to the trouble to cook something bad?"

"Well, you might," said the girl, "if you were a wicked witch. If you were a witch, you might be cooking up a potion for Halloween." She grinned. "Are you sure you're not a witch?"

"Quite," Inchbald said. "Do I look like one? And if I were a witch, as you pointed out, I should be stirring up something vile and repulsive. Eye of newt. Wing of bat. That sort of thing."

"Tooth of sloth," offered the pale lad, smiling.

"Hair of mare," added the girl.

"Toe of crow!" called out the one with the dimpled chin.

"And lizard's gizzard," cackled the girl.

"Brain of crane," said the boy with the thoughtful face.

Inchbald shuddered. The dimpled-chinned boy had planted his feet far apart and was stirring an imaginary kettle. "Ear of deer!" he shouted. "Tail of snail!"

"Snout of trout," giggled the girl.

"Throat of goat," said the thin, pale boy. He clasped his own neck and stuck his tongue out.

Inchbald raised his pudgy hands to make them stop. "My dears, I am ever so slightly squeamish. Not that I don't appreciate your wit, of course. Wouldn't you like to know what I am really cooking?"

They nodded in unison.

15

"Do come in, then. You can help me make gingerbread."

Inchbald led them through the hallway, and they crowded into the tiny kitchen. On the countertop were a large blue bowl, a package of flour, a canister labeled "Sugar," a lump of butter, a yellow box of soda, some jars, a measuring cup, the wooden spoon Inchbald had been waving about, and several small red tins.

"I think we ought to begin with introductions," Inchbald said. "I shouldn't like to cook with strangers."

The girl was called Nell. The pale face belonged to Ed. The one with the dimpled chin was Caleb. They were best friends, Nell explained. They were in the same class at Piedmont Elementary School. They lived in three houses on Arlington Court, just across the sidewalk from Inchbald. They did nearly everything together. They read the same books and played the same games. They had built a scale model of an Aztec temple.

While they talked, Inchbald set the butter to melt in a heavy pan on the stove. At one countertop, he pulled up a wooden stool and put Ed to work beating an egg together with some sugar. At the other, he let Caleb sift flour with soda, cinnamon, and ginger. He took an orange from the refrigerator and showed Nell how to rub the side of the fruit with a grater. When their voices fell silent, they enjoyed the sounds of cooking: the whirr of the eggbeater and the soft swish of the sifter. The smells of cinnamon, ginger, and orange peel made the kitchen cozier than ever. Inchbald lit the oven with a long match.

"Now comes my favorite part," Inchbald said, "when we mix it all together." Everyone took a turn with the wooden spoon, as Inchbald supervised the combining of butter, beaten egg, sugar, flour, honey, molasses, and hot water. The batter was brown and soft. Inchbald spooned it into a square pan.

"Stand back now, mates!" he said. With a flourish, he pulled open the oven door and slid the baking pan onto the center rack. As he shut the door, the clocks struck eleven. The grandfather clocks and grandmother clocks, the chimes and cuckoos and gongs rang out from every corner of Inchbald's house.

"I say, that was perfect timing, wasn't it?" Inchbald said. "Now, let me look at this recipe." He consulted a large book on the counter and nodded. "One hour. So, when the clocks strike noon, our gingerbread will be ready to come out of the oven. Isn't this fun?" They had to agree it was.

"There's only one thing that could improve this situation," Inchbald said thoughtfully.

"What?" Ed asked.

"Whipping cream. Just imagine, my dears, when we lift that gingerbread out of the oven. Risen to perfection. Steaming hot. Dark and spicy. Now that you think of it, can you even imagine it without a dollop of fresh whipped cream on top?"

They couldn't. Now that they thought of it.

"I shall have to go find some whipping cream, then," Inchbald said. "That's all there is for it. Here's what we'll do. You take your leave, and see that you return promptly at noon. I shall make everything ready."

After they had gone, Inchbald hurried upstairs to get washed and dressed. In place of Mrs. Cornblossom's apron and the flannel nightshirt, he put on a large white shirt with puffy sleeves, a pair of woolen knickers, and red suspenders. He replaced his fuzzy bunny slippers with knee-length socks and sensible walking shoes. He tugged a woolen fisherman's cap onto his bald head.

Toothbucket was in his garden, putting in tulip bulbs, when Inchbald stepped outside, consulted his pocket watch, and locked the front door. His lanky

17

neighbor looked up and gave Inchbald a slow, warm smile. "Beautiful day," he said.

"That it is," Inchbald agreed. "I say, Toothbucket, have you got any whipping cream?"

"Whipping cream? No, I don't have any. I'm sorry."

"Oh, it's quite all right, my dear fellow. Don't look so sad. I have more than enough time to walk to the store. A bit of a stroll will do me good. And when I get back, you must join me, and our three little neighbors—Caleb, Ed, and Nell—for a spot of gingerbread."

Toothbucket nodded. It occurred to him, now, that he had forgotten to eat breakfast. A spot of gingerbread— better yet, three or four big slabs of gingerbread—would suit him well.

Off went Inchbald, down the sidewalk and through the gate. He strode briskly, in his knickers and suspenders, to the corner store, where he bought a small container of whipping cream. The clerk put the whipping cream into a paper bag, and Inchbald carried it back to Arlington Court. At his doorstep, he checked his pocket watch once again. It was fifteen minutes before noon. Just enough time, thought Inchbald agreeably, to whip up the cream, brew a pot of tea, and set the table.

Even though the door was shut, the smell of baking gingerbread wafted through the keyhole. Inchbald sniffed and sighed happily. He dug into the pocket of his knickers for the key.

It was not there. Nor was it in his other pocket. It was not in the pocket of his shirt. It was not in the paper bag with the whipping cream. Inchbald set the bag on the doorstep and searched again. He took out his watch, his coin purse, and his lucky penny. There was no key.

Just then, the three children came tumbling out of a door across the court, waving and laughing. "Is it time?" they called. "Is it gingerbread time?"

"Oh dear, oh dear," Inchbald said. He turned to them and cried, "I've lost the key! We can't get in!"

"We'll look for it!" said Caleb. The three went hunting. They searched every square of sidewalk between Inchbald's door and the neighborhood store. Nell even went inside and asked the clerk if a key had been dropped. But they found no key. When they returned, Inchbald was still on the porch, wringing his hands and looking more and more distressed.

Toothbucket, who had just washed his hands and face, came out of his house and through the garden to Inchbald's porch. He could tell immediately that something was wrong.

"Toothbucket, we have a terrible problem!" Inchbald sputtered. "I've locked the door and lost the key! Whatever shall we do?" He looked at his pocket watch. "It will be twelve o'clock in a few minutes!"

Slowly, Toothbucket scratched his head. He pulled his beard. He seemed to be thinking very hard.

"What is it, Toothbucket? Have you got an idea?"

"Mrs. Cornblossom," said Toothbucket.

"What about Mrs. Cornblossom?"

"I seem to remember that Mrs. Cornblossom gave me a key to her house, one time," Toothbucket said.

"How fortunate!" Inchbald squealed. He clapped his fat little hands. "We are saved by Mrs. Cornblossom! Toothbucket, do go get the key she gave you. It's nearly time!"

"I can't," Toothbucket said. "I've forgotten where I put it."

"Surely you can remember if you try," Inchbald said. "Think, man, think!"

Toothbucket thought. Everyone waited. Inchbald chewed his fingertips. Caleb and Ed jostled each other and bounced up and down. Nell sat on the bottom step and rested her dark head between her hands, as if to help Toothbucket think. The smell of gingerbread seeped through the keyhole and out the cracks under the door.

From inside the house, the clocks began to sound.

"No, no, no!" Inchbald shook his fists as if he could command the machines to be still and hold back time. But they kept chiming and gonging. The cuckoo bird sounded its doleful call—twelve times. They heard the bong-bong-bong of the biggest grandfather clock—twelve times. Inchbald put his hands over his ears.

The boys looked at one another. What could they do? Ed, thinking to make one last search for the key on the sidewalk, ran down the steps. Suddenly he pointed up toward the top of the house. "Look!" he yelled.

They all rushed out to the sidewalk to look. Ed was pointing at a small window on the third story of Inchbald's house. There was a face behind the window.

For a split second, hardly enough time to think it but enough time to feel a surge of happiness, Toothbucket thought the face was Mrs. Cornblossom's. But then it moved, and he recognized Cocobean.

Cocobean meowed. Down on the sidewalk, they could hear her. They watched as she pushed the window from the inside. It swung outward. The cat leaped out of the window and onto the roof. She walked along the steep roof, dangerously close to the edge. She looked down at all of them and gave another pitiful meow.

"Cocobean, stay right there," Toothbucket said softly. "I will come up and get you." Faster than he had ever moved, in anyone's memory, Toothbucket loped away to get the ladder in his basement. He returned soon, and propped it against the side of Inchbald's house.

Cocobean peered over the edge at Toothbucket. "Don't move, Cocobean," he pleaded. He started to climb the ladder, but someone tugged at his pants leg.

"Toothbucket, take me with you." It was Nell. "You see, I think I can squeeze through the window and unlock the front door!"

Toothbucket looked at the small girl. He looked up at Cocobean. "All right," he said. He scooped Nell into one arm, and started up the ladder again.

Nell watched the ground get further away. Of course she had been up this high, in her own attic, but never outside. Never in the arm of a big, tall man, with the autumn breeze blowing through her hair and her friends down below, watching her.

They reached the roof. Cocobean, waiting patiently, gave a squeak of pleasure. Toothbucket helped Nell to the window, and watched as she clambered inside. Then, taking Cocobean tenderly in the arm that had carried Nell, he made his way down again.

Meanwhile, Nell raced through the house: down to the second floor, down to the first. She took the stairs with familiar leaps, for they were exactly like the stairs in her own home. She unlocked the door. They all came tumbling in—Inchbald first, then Caleb and Ed, and finally Toothbucket, still clutching the naughty Cocobean.

Inchbald made a dash for the kitchen. He grabbed a potholder from the drawer next to the stove and eased the hot gingerbread out of the oven.

"Hallelujah!" he exclaimed. The gingerbread was not burned. He took off his cap and began to fan his face. A small metal object flew out from inside the cap and landed on the floor with a pinging sound. It was the key to the front door.

With Caleb's help, Inchbald beat the cream until it stood in high and fluffy peaks. They ate gingerbread until the pan was empty, and the cat Cocobean had a saucer of whipped cream, all her own.

CHAPTER FOUR:
THE STORM

Of all the things Toothbucket loved to do, his favorite was taking walks. Toothbucket's long legs took him all over the town. Sometimes he walked to the farmer's market with a large burlap bag, and brought it home bulging with apples and turnips and rutabaga. Sometimes he walked to a bakery on the West Side and returned with a round loaf of rye bread studded with caraway seeds.

On most of his walks, however, Toothbucket simply went wherever his feet wandered and looked at whatever there was to see. In his faded overalls, long beard swaying with each step, he traveled the main streets and the alleys, through the tidy neighborhoods where houses stood in neat rows and up narrow hollows where tumbledown shanties perched every which way on the hillsides.

Toothbucket always walked alone, but he did not feel lonely. He made up little bits of songs as he went. Or he thought about the garden, or about a book he was reading, or about the dripping faucet he meant to fix as soon as he got back home, the one that had been dripping for more than a year. Sometimes he didn't think about anything at all.

On a day in late autumn, he found himself craving a wooded, quiet place. Happily, a woodland trail wound up the mountain not far from Arlington Court. To reach it, he walked across the bridge that spanned the wide river and down a narrow street where no one lived anymore. There, among a mass of raspberry brambles and honeysuckle vines beside a stone wall, trees arched over an opening. From that place, a path led upward. The climb was not steep, for the trail changed directions, winding its way back and forth. It ended at a stone stairway that was carpeted with moss and almost overgrown with vines.

The stairway ascended to what had once been the kitchen garden of a grand mansion. Now it was an abandoned place, full of mystery and sadness and a strange, still, holy feeling. Four bulging columns guarded the doors of the mansion, but the doors were boarded shut. Ivy grew over the windows. In the evening, small graceful bats flew in and out of a broken pane on the third floor.

There was a stone bench in the garden, beneath a sarvis tree that produced a froth of white flowers every spring. Where the hill sloped away on the north side, Toothbucket was accustomed to digging each April among a large patch of aromatic ramps.

Now it was November. The sky hung low and grey, as if a heavy woolen blanket lay over the town. From habit, Toothbucket lowered himself onto the stone bench to rest for a few minutes before walking wherever his legs would wander next.

As he sat, he thought of Mrs. Cornblossom. Thanksgiving had passed. It was the first Thanksgiving in years that they had not dined together. More than two months had passed since her disappearance. He did not know if he would ever see her again. Worse than that, he could not bring his friend's face to mind. Instead of a clear picture, Toothbucket could remember only a blurred image of the old woman. In fact, all he could remember clearly were her socks.

Mrs. Cornblossom wore nubby wool stockings that looked as if she had knitted them herself from corn tassels. Inside her house and on the porch, she wore them without shoes. When she went into the garden, she slipped on a pair of mud-caked clogs that rested beside the door.

Even in the garden, however, she wore a skirt. Her favorite, Toothbucket recalled, was a broomstick skirt with three tiers, made of cotton homespun in blue and yellow plaid. It was the sort of garment that could billow and whip in a good wind, though never enough to reveal her knees. Mrs. Cornblossom must have had knees under the skirt, but Toothbucket had never seen them.

What he had seen were her hands. They were square, sensible hands, the fingers knobby and rather large. Her fingernails were yellow. Toothbucket could remember seeing a line of tiny red wounds that ran across her knuckles after she had been berry picking. Mrs. Cornblossom's hands were not pretty, but kind and capable. With them, she could open a stubborn jar of canned tomatoes, or stroke the soft spot under Cocobean's chin, or tie the strings of her apron behind her back before baking bread.

Her hands were always busy. When she wasn't kneading bread or working in the garden, she sometimes sat on the porch with Toothbucket to chat. At these times, he knew, she would slip her hand into the pocket of her faded corduroy jacket and rub her favorite stone.

For as long as he had known her, Mrs. Cornblossom had carried the same stone in her pocket. It was about the diameter of a medium-sized buckeye, but flatter. It was roughly round, but with a bulge on one edge, as if it had wished to sprout a limb but had gotten only as far as putting forth a bony nubbin. The stone was smooth and grey except for a spattering of incised pockmarks and wiggly lines on one side. It looked as if tiny worms had left behind trails of short journeys, or as if someone had gone to the trouble to carve a message into the stone, but in a language long lost to human understanding. Mrs. Cornblossom liked to look at the markings and wonder about what they might mean, although her curiosity was not real.

"Even if I could figure it out, Toothbucket," she had once told him, "it isn't likely to say anything more important than what those bluets by the sidewalk can tell me, is it? Still, I like to have it about me. I like its dear shape."

Toothbucket knew the story of the stone. Mrs. Cornblossom had picked it up on a beach, the day of a total eclipse of the sun. She and Mr. Cornblossom, whom Toothbucket had never met, had traveled for two whole days to stand on a particular bluff overlooking Lake Erie. There they watched as the moon passed in front of the sun and the world turned purple and cool for a few magical minutes.

"I was always doing things like that, back then," she said. "Always going off somewhere." After she said that, she looked up at the treetops above the attics of Arlington Court. Her blue eyes shone, and her face softened into an expression that was both happy and sad.

Her face! Her face! Like sunlight moving in a dappled forest, the image of Mrs. Cornblossom's face was with him suddenly. But by the time Toothbucket realized it, in a rush of gratitude and joy, the precious image was already dissolving.

A tear slipped down Toothbucket's cheek, but he

was smiling, too. And, though he could not see his own face, it was beautiful.

The stone bench had chilled his bones. The sky, Toothbucket saw, had turned a dark blue color. The days were getting shorter, but it was not time for sundown. Toothbucket needed no clock to tell him it was not yet noon. Was this an eclipse, like the one Mrs. Cornblossom had watched when she was young?

Leaves swirled around Toothbucket as he unbent his long frame and stood. He pulled at his shirt collar and wished he had brought a scarf. The wind was rising, and it was cold—not the fragrant breeze of autumn, but the hard, sharp wind of winter. Toothbucket started downhill. There would be no more wandering today; he wanted to get back to Arlington Court as soon as he could.

As if obeying some signal only they could hear, trees that had clung to their leaves until this day released them all at once. They whirled in funnels and cartwheels, chasing Toothbucket as he hurried toward the first switchback. Large drops of cold rain began to break on his head. The sky blackened. The trees waved their branches and made shrieking sounds. The wind began to howl through the small forest. The creek ran muddy and fast.

Then something happened that made Toothbucket stop. From behind him came a bright flash followed by a tremendous cracking sound. He turned just in time to see the top of the sarvis tree, with smoke pouring from its stricken center, give a great groan and split slowly away from its trunk. It fell with an earth-shuddering thud on top of the stone bench.

The sky cracked again. The rain fell harder, soaking Toothbucket's clothes. He looked back once more at the smoldering sarvis. Then he began to run. He ran in great sloshing leaps, faster and faster. The dark world became a blur around him. He was almost at the bottom of the hill when he fell.

He tumbled over a stone embankment and landed face-down in the creek. The water was icy.

Mud-covered and bruised, he dragged himself out and climbed the bank. Now Toothbucket went on at a slightly slower pace. He felt his body freezing, and each step was more difficult than the last. The wind screeched and bit his ears. His sodden beard clung to his face like a large frozen fish. Water ran in a small stream from the tip of his nose, and some of the drops were tears.

By the time he reached the gate to Arlington Court, Toothbucket's hands were so cold that he could hardly unlatch the gate. Shuddering and coughing, he made his way along the sidewalk. But instead of proceeding to his own dark house, he pulled himself up the steps to Inchbald's porch, where the porch light burned in a welcoming way. With one cold-stiffened finger, he pressed on the bell for a long time.

Inchbald appeared. When he saw Toothbucket, he blinked and gasped, "What on earth have you done to yourself?" Then he opened the door and waved his friend inside. Toothbucket stood silently while Inchbald rushed to bring towels, exclaimed over the mud and a nasty tear in the knee of Toothbucket's overalls, put on a kettle of water to boil, and went to find some warm old clothes for Toothbucket to put on in place of his wet ones. He came back with a pair of pants that, while they fit around his waist, reached only as far as Toothbucket's knees, and a corduroy jacket.

Toothbucket recognized the jacket. He reached his thawing hand into the pocket. The stone was there. Its off-round shape was unmistakable. He felt for, and found, the pockmarks and squiggles. For a moment, his weary brain puzzled over the shape. Where would Mrs. Cornblossom go without taking her favorite stone?

In slow motion, Toothbucket's heart, like the heart of the sarvis tree, groaned and broke.

The kettle whistled. Inchbald scurried off to make tea. When he had set the tea to steep, he went to the bureau in the back room and pulled out clean flannel sheets and woolen blankets to make a bed on the sofa. When Toothbucket was settled down and tucked in, Inchbald went back to the kitchen to fetch the tea.

But Toothbucket was huddled under the blankets, and did not reply when Inchbald said, "Tea time!" Nor did he stir, a few minutes later, when the clocks chimed all around him. Inchbald sighed, picked up the teapot, put out the light, and went to gather the ingredients for chicken soup.

CHAPTER FIVE:
PORCH MUSIC

Ed was bored. The rain had begun a little after noon, accompanied by a brilliant flash of lightning and a loud clap of thunder that followed almost immediately afterwards. Reluctantly, he came inside and made himself a sandwich. Now the rest of a rainy November Saturday stretched ahead of him.

The house, too, felt dim and lonely. There was no one with whom to play a game or put together a jigsaw puzzle. His friend Caleb had gone with his family to Pittsburgh to stay the whole Thanksgiving weekend with Caleb's aunt and uncle. He wouldn't be home until late on Sunday evening. And Nell was spending the holiday weekend with her grandmother, who lived on the other side of town.

At least Ed had both a mother and a father—he was luckier than Nell in that way, he guessed—but his father was far away, and his absence was a constant ache. Ed's father had gone off on a Navy ship, more than six months ago, to fight in the war. When he left, he had said to Ed, "You'll be the man of the house while I'm gone, son. I know you'll be a good helper for your mother."

He was a good helper. When he came home from school every day, he found on the kitchen table a note from his mother, along with a snack she had prepared for him—a slice of banana bread wrapped in foil, a couple of peanut butter cookies, or perhaps an apple and some graham crackers. He would get a glass of milk from the refrigerator and settle himself at the kitchen table to read his mother's message. He knew there would be one or two chores to do, and he knew that there would be a loving postscript. She might have written, "Your daddy would be proud of you!" or "I love you, Snuggle Bug," or "How about pizza for dinner?"

There was no note today, of course, because there was no school. In fact, his mother usually didn't go to work on Saturdays. This morning, however, the telephone had interrupted their lazy breakfast of pancakes with maple syrup.

"Oh, dear. Of course I will," Ed's mother said, after listening for a time. She hung up the telephone and sighed. "Honey, I need to fill in for Naomi," she told Ed. "She's put her back out and can't come in to work today."

"It's okay, Mom," Ed replied, although it wasn't okay, not really. She had promised Ed that they would spend the afternoon finishing the Christmas gift they had made, together, for his father. It was a wonderful gift, a handmade chess set. Ed's mother had come up with the idea of using the knobbed tops of clothespins for the chess pieces. Ed himself had devised the various embellishments that identified rooks, knights, bishops, queens, and kings. Yesterday afternoon he had painted them, one group white and one black. His mother had told him they would apply the final touch, a coat of varnish, today, so that they could mail the gift on Monday morning. Ed had been looking forward to it more than he'd realized. He could varnish the chess pieces by himself, he knew, but he didn't want to. He wanted them to do it together.

"We'll find time tomorrow afternoon," she said to him. "Oh, honey, I really am sorry. It can't be helped."

"I know," he sighed.

"And, while the varnish is drying," his mother continued, "we'll start decorating the house for Christmas. Why don't you go up into the attic sometime today and bring down the box of candles and the crèche?"

"And the ornaments?" Ed said, brightening at the prospect. The thought of a twinkling Christmas tree, and of hanging all the ornaments they saved from year to year, cheered him considerably.

"Not yet. I think we'd better wait another week or so to put up our tree. But there's no reason we can't hang a wreath on the door and decorate the mantel. And we'll have some hot apple cider spiced with cinnamon."

Then, pulling on her coat, she had left for work, and he was alone.

Ed finished eating his sandwich, washed the knife and plate he had used, and put the loaf of bread back into the breadbox. As he climbed the stairs to the attic, he picked up his guitar and carried it with him.

Mrs. Cornblossom had given him the guitar back in the spring of the year, about a week after Ed's father left for the war. Ed loved the guitar, not only because it was Mrs. Cornblossom's gift but also because it reminded him of his favorite season in Arlington Court—summertime, the season of porch music.

In fact, depending upon the weather, porch music might start as early as sometime in April. At the end of a warm day, Mrs. Cornblossom would bring her banjo out to the front porch and begin to play. The twilight would turn lavender, then deep blue, while she strummed and plinked. She wasn't a fast, bluegrass banjo picker. Hers was a gentle music, the notes silver and separate like the blinking of fireflies, one after another, or like the sun making ropy patterns, over and over, on smooth stones at the bottom of a shallow creek.

And, whenever Mrs. Cornblossom played her banjo, Ed found himself, sooner or later, quite without knowing how he had come to be there, sitting on the bottom step of her porch, rocking his head slightly and tapping his foot in rhythm with the tune.

Often Toothbucket joined them, bringing a battered fiddle. Toothbucket liked to sing, and he knew the words to many songs. He sang about Old Joe Clark and John Henry, Liza Jane and Pretty Polly; about blue-eyed Davy, who got drunk on chicken and gravy; about groundhogs and hoecakes and chickens crowing on Sourwood Mountain. Sometimes Mrs. Cornblossom added a harmony. Occasionally, she put down the banjo and the two of them sang, a cappella, a long ballad about a young man who pined away and died for love, all because the hard-hearted Barbara Allen wouldn't marry him.

Toothbucket's voice was true-pitched but raspy— like something extruded from a cement mixer, Ed thought privately, liquid but full of gravel and grit. Mrs. Cornblossom had the wavery, papery voice of an old woman, and it floated above Toothbucket's like a moth fluttering about in a dim room. Ed knew that no one would call them professional singers, but he liked the way they sounded. Their harmonies were meant for a porch at dusk, not a concert hall.

It was on one of those spring nights, after such a song, that Mrs. Cornblossom had brought out the guitar. She didn't make a ceremony of it; in fact, she didn't say anything at all, merely placed it in Ed's hands.

"I can't play it," he told her, but she appeared not to hear him. She sat back down on her porch swing, picked up her banjo, and began to pluck out the familiar notes of "I Don't Like No Railroad Man."

"I don't like no railroad fool," Toothbucket sang the end of the song. "Railroad fool got a head like a mule. I don't like no railroad fool." With a squeaky flourish from the old fiddle, the song was ended.

"I can't play it," Ed repeated, and held the guitar out to Mrs. Cornblossom. His cheeks were burning. He wished furiously that he could play it.

"Oh, that doesn't matter," said Mrs. Cornblossom. "It's been so long since that old guitar made music, I thought it would do it good just to have someone hold it."

So he held the guitar, in the way that he thought he had seen real musicians do, for the rest of the evening, until Toothbucket yawned and stretched and said it was high time for him to take himself off to bed.

Mrs. Cornblossom played one more tune, sweet and slow. Then, in the darkness, she said, "I could teach you a chord or two. You'd pick it up easy."

In his arms, the guitar was warm, and it seemed to fit along his body, as if it felt comfortable to be near him.

"Okay," he said.

She showed him where to put his fingers. It felt awkward, but he willed them to stay in place. "Now strum," she said. "See how it sounds."

It sounded good. He strummed again.

"That's a G chord," Mrs. Cornblossom said.

Within a week, he had learned three more chords. Little by little, the fingerings began to feel natural, and he found that he could follow along with quite a few of the old-time songs Mrs. Cornblossom and Toothbucket played. Mrs. Cornblossom was delighted, she said, by his steady progress. She added that she had rarely met a youngster whose sense of harmony was so intuitive.

"Harmony is a gift," she told him one evening. "I declare, Ed, you were born to make music. This old guitar of Mr. Cornblossom's has been waiting for someone like you. I'm certain he would want you to have it." And, although Ed's mother had at first protested that he could not accept such a valuable thing, Mrs. Cornblossom prevailed. Ed inherited Mr. Cornblossom's guitar.

Now he sat on a wooden stool beside the attic window, strumming softly and looking down into the courtyard. The attic was Ed's favorite spot. Up here, he felt like a bird hidden in a leafy tree. Looking down from the window of the front gable, he could see the whole length of the sidewalk and most of the porches that flanked it.

Today, though, there was not much to see. Since the rain had started, nobody was about, not even the cat Cocobean. Earlier, he had watched Inchbald come out to shake a rag rug vigorously from the side of his porch. The little man had shivered, wrinkled his nose at the rain, and scurried back indoors.

The rain fell harder. The sound of raindrops on the attic roof reminded him of Mrs. Cornblossom's banjo, and he felt a strong pang of sorrow. Mrs. Cornblossom had been gone for many weeks. Not as long as his father had been away, but there had been letters from his father, and telephone calls. Mrs. Cornblossom had simply disappeared, and no one had heard from her. Ed was beginning to feel that he would never see her again.

The raindrops pelted against the roof. Twang! Ping! Plunk! There was a strange music in the sound. He perked up his ears and began to follow it. The fingers of his left hand found their positions along the fretted fingerboard of the guitar. Slowly at first and then with increasing confidence, he began to harmonize with the rain. It was a plaintive melody, like one of the old Appalachian ballads Toothbucket loved to sing, and the chords switched from major to minor, jigging back and forth like a stream that couldn't decide where it wanted to flow.

And there were words to the song—or rather, a chorus. It was not a refrain that Ed had ever heard, he was sure of that. Yet he could not quite believe that he was making it up, for these lyrics were the old-fashioned, tender words of some ancient lament:

And where ye have gone, there is no one can tell
Farewell, my darling, farewell.

He tried singing the lines, but his voice broke on the word "darling" and trailed off to a whisper. "Farewell," he breathed. "Farewell."

Ed put down his guitar. It was time to find the Christmas decorations, which his mother kept in boxes in the opposite corner of the attic. He hoped she would be home soon. He would be glad to see her.

As he straightened up, a movement outside caught his eye. Through the blotchy, rain-spattered attic window, he saw Toothbucket—but could that stiff, elderly figure be Toothbucket?—stumbling along the sidewalk, as drenched as a drowned rat. He stopped in front of Inchbald's house, took hold of the railing, heaved himself up to the porch, and pushed on the doorbell. Ed could see his shoulders shaking.

Ed watched the door open. Inchbald's surprised face appeared, and he said something, although Ed couldn't hear anything but the rain. Then Inchbald ushered Toothbucket inside and closed the door.

CHAPTER SIX:
ANIMAL TRACKS

Underneath two woolen blankets, one of which was drawn up above his ears on both sides of his dimpled chin, Caleb was wide awake. He knew it was not yet morning, but his bedroom was filled with something like light—a silvery, cool glow. And there was a smell. Not a strong smell, but a clean odor with a hint of a metallic sparkle. He sniffed deeply, and remembered what it meant. Snow!

He threw aside the blankets and ran to the window. In the circle of light from the streetlamp at the end of Arlington Court, snowflakes whirled and glinted. Caleb bounced up and down on his bare feet.

He hurried to pull on long underwear, his thickest wool sweater, his warmest trousers, and his heaviest woolen socks. In stocking feet, he tiptoed into the kitchen. No one else was awake. He turned on the small lamp on the kitchen table. The clock, ticking contentedly in its place on top of the refrigerator, said half past six. He fetched the tin of oatmeal from the pantry.

Carefully, he struck a match and lit the front burner of the stove. Beginning with Inchbald's gingerbread lesson a few months before, Caleb had discovered a keen interest in cooking. And, after she had watched him do it a dozen times, his mother had given him permission to light the burners by himself. But he was still wary of the ring of blue fire that flared so suddenly, with a sound of something being torn.

He measured a full cup of water, poured it into a saucepan, and set the pan over the flame. When it was boiling, he turned the flame as low as he could, watching from the side to make sure it didn't flicker and disappear. Then he sprinkled in the oatmeal, added a pinch of salt, and covered the saucepan. He consulted the clock and calculated the time it would take for the oatmeal to cook.

"Now," he whispered, "comes the fun part." Inchbald had taught him this, too, one afternoon when he showed Caleb how he concocted the buttery scones he sometimes served for afternoon tea.

"Cooking, my young fellow, is an act of creation. Or should be." Inchbald's round face crinkled into a mischievous grin and his eyes gleamed as he said this. "Of course you must pay attention to basic proportions. You simply cannot bake a good yeast bread without flour and water and a pinch of something sweet, that sort of thing. But, beyond that, the possibilities are nearly limitless." Inchbald threw his arms out expansively. "Spices! Herbs! Nuts, berries, a dash of lime or good liqueur! Any and all of these can transform the ordinary into the exquisite." He lingered over the word "exquisite," pinching the thumb and forefinger of his right hand together and wiggling them in the air, closing his eyes and drawing in a long breath. "You must experiment, my boy."

"What if it doesn't work out?"

"Oh, there will be failures, without a doubt. If you are bold and joyful in your creativity, there will be unmitigated disasters. You will produce inedible catastrophes!" Here he cackled as if the prospect brought him great delight. "That is part and parcel of the learning process. If you never fail gloriously, you will have very little hope of succeeding stupendously."

There had been failures. Caleb had learned, for instance, that nobody in his household—with the exception of Lucy, the family's old and patient golden retriever—would eat meatballs that had been dyed bright blue with food coloring.

After the blue meatball incident, Caleb's mother suggested that he confine his bold experiments to his own bowls of oatmeal.

And so began what Caleb's father dubbed the Oatmeal Odyssey. Caleb hunted through the cupboards, the pantry, the spice rack. Each day he added different ingredients to the basics, oatmeal and water, and he kept notes about which ones made the oatmeal taste better and which he didn't care to try a second time. Dried cranberries were wonderful. Cranberries and bits of peeled apple, with a pinch of cinnamon and few drops of vanilla, approached Inchbald's "exquisite" rating. Bananas were delicious, as long as you waited until the oatmeal was almost fully cooked before slicing them into the simmering saucepan. Raisins were good, bits of date even better. Chopped walnuts were superb.

On this morning, however, Caleb was too impatient to concentrate on creating an original recipe. Almost absentmindedly, he dropped a handful of salted peanuts and some raisins into the saucepan. His attention strayed to the window, where the grey light of a winter morning was gradually replacing the dusty blue of a winter night. The snow was still falling, although less thickly, and it lay luxuriously on every surface. A glistening blanket, at least three inches thick, covered bushes and branches, sidewalks and steps. He could hardly wait to plunge into the wondrous whiteness.

While the oatmeal bubbled, he collected his hat and

mittens, then sat on the rug beside the woodstove, next to Lucy. He rubbed behind her ears, and she showed her appreciation by laying her head in his lap.

"Don't you want to come play in the snow, Lucy?" he said quietly.

She thumped her tail as if she remembered her youthful days of romping outside in winter weather. Once, Lucy had loved to burrow her nose into mounds of freshly fallen snow and fling it about, yapping wildly. But now she went out into the cold reluctantly, and she was ready to come back indoors within a few minutes, whereupon she would walk slowly in a circle on the rug, finally settling her old bones with a deep sigh, as if she had endured an ordeal and was grateful to have come through it, one more time, undamaged and alive.

From the back of the house came the sound of a door opening and closing softly. Caleb's mother padded into the kitchen in her purple bathrobe. "Mmmm, the oatmeal smells good," she said. "It woke me up." She bent, combed her fingers through his tangled hair, and smiled.

"Morning, Mom," he said, getting up. He gave his oatmeal a final stir, turned off the flame, and spooned it into a waiting bowl.

"You're awake early for a Saturday morning," she said.

"Look outside, Mom. It's snowing!"

"I know," she said. "It's beautiful, isn't it?"

Caleb didn't reply; his mouth was full of oatmeal. The need to be outdoors, out in the snow, was calling him urgently. Impatiently, he blew on the next spoonful of oatmeal to cool it. His mother busied herself with the coffeepot.

A tapping at the kitchen window caused both of them to look up. There, waving a stick and grinning broadly, was Ed. Caleb waved back, and went to open the door.

Stamping his feet to knock the snow off his boots, Ed came inside. "Isn't it amazing?" he laughed. He took off his glasses and swiped at them with a mitten.

"Let's go up to the old mansion," Caleb said. "Can we go, Mom? Please? There won't be many cars out on a day like this."

"Well...." Caleb's mother considered. "All right. But you must be careful crossing the streets, and especially the bridge, because it may be icy."

"We will," they promised in unison.

"And, Ed, I think we'd better ask your mother's permission for this expedition, too. I'll call her on the telephone."

Soon it was all arranged, and Caleb's mother had made peanut butter and jelly sandwiches for the boys. "Just in case you get stranded in a snowdrift," she said, winking at them.

Caleb, wrapped in layers of underwear and sweater and jacket, could barely contain himself. "Let's go!" he urged his friend. The next moment, in a whirl of snow and laughter, the two boys were out the door.

Outside, the whole world seemed to hold its breath. The snowfall had nearly ended; only a few glittery flakes floated out of the sky now. No traffic moved in the streets, and the cars they did see were no longer cars, but soft, rounded shapes that resembled large, sleeping animals.

Ahead of them, the expanse of the neighborhood park lay pristine and trackless. It was almost a shame to disturb it—and yet, it was irresistible. They headed across it diagonally, along a sidewalk barely distinguishable from the lawns on either side. The park was an etching, every tree limb picked out in white. Ed scooped up a handful of snow from one end of the seesaw, threw it up in the air, and spun around in a shower of spangles. They threw snowballs, first at one another and then at a knob of burl on a large oak tree, testing their skill at aiming and throwing.

Soon they were crossing the river, the water below them choppy and dark. When they had come almost to the middle of the bridge, Ed called, "Look! Barges!" Indeed, six enormous barges, two abreast, moved slowly toward them, guided by a tugboat. The boys stood at the very center of the bridge until the huge slabs, each bearing its own mountain of snow-dusted coal, slid beneath them. As always, Caleb felt a momentary dizziness, as if it were the bridge that was moving, with the two of them atop it, instead of the barges below. They lobbed snowballs into the barges, marveling at how long it took for them to fall the distance from bridge to barge. A furl of foamy wake fanned out beside the great vessels and rolled toward the river's edge.

Last of all came the tugboat. They waved and waved, and were rewarded with a mighty blast from the boat's horn—a sound that ripped through the snowy silence of the valley and vibrated their very bones. Whooping with both terror and delight, they went running, slipping and sliding all the way, to the other end of the bridge.

They made their way along the stone wall, its mantle of vines and ivy outlined with snow, and began the climb along the wooded path. Both boys fell silent now. This moment of passing from city into forest always gave Caleb a church-like feeling, and the hemlocks towering on either side seemed especially sacred when their branches bore heavy white offerings. From time to time a clump of snow plopped to the ground. All around them was a sifting of colored light as individual flakes, each a tiny prism, drifted down.

Beneath the hemlocks, the cover of snow was not so deep. Caleb kept his eyes on the ground, searching for animal tracks.

Mrs. Cornblossom had taught him to look at animal tracks; she had learned from her husband, whom Caleb had never met because Mr. Cornblossom had been dead for years and years.

"Mr. Cornblossom was a full-blooded Cherokee," she had told Caleb one day, as he sat watching her while she swept her front porch. "He was the most careful observer I ever knew. I'd have gone into any wilderness with him, and not a moment's hesitation." She had smiled down at her broom, perhaps remembering a particular excursion into one wilderness or another.

"My dad says we have some Cherokee ancestors," Caleb remarked.

"Ah," Mrs. Cornblossom replied. She stopped sweeping, contemplated his face, and nodded her head slowly. "You know, that doesn't surprise me at all. You've got a sharp eye for a boy your age, and an ear for listening. I've thought so for some time."

Caleb said nothing, but inwardly he felt a warmth blooming somewhere in the region of his heart. Mrs. Cornblossom had a way of making him feel good about himself.

"Have you seen the opossum tracks behind Arlington Court?" she asked.

Caleb shook his head. Propping the broom in the corner, she motioned for him to follow her. They went through her house and out the back door, where Arlington Court's row of back stoops faced a narrow alley.

"I think he was trying to find something good to eat in the garbage can," she explained, crouching over some patterns in a skin of dried mud near her stoop.

"How can you tell it was an opossum, and not a squirrel or a raccoon?" Caleb wondered aloud. "I think raccoons get into garbage cans, too."

"Look at this." She beckoned, and he bent down beside her. "Here, on his hind feet, he's got a sort of thumb that points out sideways, just as our thumbs do." She held up her own hand to demonstrate. "No other animal in these parts has a thumb like that. And do you see this long, thin mark? It shows that he was dragging his tail."

That was how it started. Caleb took to animal tracking with a fervor. He borrowed books from the library. He scouted the neighborhood and the wooded trail to the abandoned mansion, looking for evidence of deer mice, chipmunks, owls, rabbits, and squirrels. Once he saw a great blue heron at the river's edge and later found its huge, pronged tracks, spanning a full five inches from front to back, in a sandy place between some rocks. He began to carry a small notebook for making drawings.

Mrs. Cornblossom tutored him. Although she was far too old to go hiking about in the woods, she said, she was always happy to look at his drawings and listen to descriptions of what he had seen. Sometimes she could identify an animal from a mere detail. The pebbled texture of a porcupine's paw was fixed in her memory, and the beaver's webbed hind feet.

From Mrs. Cornblossom, he learned to look not only for tracks in mud and snow, but also for other evidence of animals and their habits. He began to find it everywhere. A pile of nut shells. A mound of pellet-shaped droppings. A scattering of feathers. All of these signs had stories to tell. And all told of a teeming population that lived and traveled and ate and slept and died, mostly unnoticed by humans, all around him.

"The whole earth is a web," Mrs. Cornblossom said,

46

"and every creature is important. In the old days, as Mr. Cornblossom used to say, when we could understand what the animals and plants said, there was harmony and balance in the world."

"Animals could talk?" Caleb sputtered.

"Of course they could. They still talk—and sing, and tell stories, and cry. It's just that we don't understand them."

"Do you understand them?"

"Hardly ever," she said. And, for a moment, he thought Mrs. Cornblossom was going to cry. Instead, she brushed her hands on her apron and said, "Now, you must be getting hungry. How about a piece of pumpkin pie?"

Caleb put his memories aside. From a clearing up ahead, Ed was calling to him, "Here's something! What do you think this is?" Caleb hurried to catch up with his friend.

Together they examined some impressions in the snow. The tracks made a distinct pattern. There were two oval shapes side by side, with a smaller oval just behind them, creating a triangle. Trailing behind the triangular pattern was a second small oval. The set repeated itself twice before disappearing beneath a jumble of brush.

"Do you see any claw marks?" Caleb said.

Ed bent closer to scrutinize the tracks. "No, I don't think so."

Hunkered together in the snow, they looked around, checking for other signs in the area nearby.

"Look at those twigs," Caleb said.

"It looks like someone's cut them off clean, with a pair of scissors," Ed replied.

"A rabbit, I think. Probably a cottontail. They have sharp teeth."

They walked on. Within a short distance they

47

recognized the tracks of deer; even Ed could immediately identify the deep, two-toed marks. They found the meandering trails of several dogs and a straighter line of clawed tracks that might have belonged to a red fox.

Approaching the top of the hill, where the old mansion overlooked the river and town, they found the neat paw prints of a domestic cat and, nearby, a dead field mouse. Beside it, a few drops of blood seeped into the snow.

"Poor little mousie," Ed whispered, pulling his hand out of a mitten to stroke the small, still form.

"Maybe we shouldn't touch it," Caleb cautioned. "It's someone's lunch, I suppose."

The word "lunch" reminded them of their sandwiches. They sprinted for their favorite resting spot, a stone bench beneath a small tree, and were surprised and dismayed to find the tree broken and blackened, its graceful branches flung down at awkward angles. Worse, its fall had cracked the stone bench into two pieces.

So they settled themselves on a short set of steps that led from the outside of the mansion to its cellar. They ate quickly, not speaking. The sandwiches tasted good, but sitting still made Caleb realize how cold the weather was. He was ready to go home, and he began to think about how good a steaming mug of cocoa would taste. Apparently Ed was cold, too, for he got up, stamped his feet, and said, "What do you say? Home again?"

"Yes," Caleb agreed. But, as he stood, he saw another set of tracks in the snow, marks that their own boots had almost obliterated. They were not animal tracks, but prints left by someone's shoes. Just a person, walking toward the cellar of the mansion. But it had been today, or the tracks would have been covered by falling snow. And something about these particular footprints made him stop and look more closely.

"Come on," Ed said. "I'm getting chilled, just standing around."

"Go on ahead," Caleb replied. "I'll catch up with you in a minute." As Ed began to walk down the pathway, Caleb knelt in the snow and stared intently at the footprints.

The impressions were smaller than a man's shoe; a woman or a child had left them. The soles of the shoes had left a series of wavy lines embossed in the snow. And near the outer edge of the right footprint was a smooth, almost circular shape where something, a bit of tar perhaps, had become lodged in the sole but never pried out. Caleb was sure he had seen these footprints before. He squinted his eyes shut, trying to remember where.

It came to him. Of course. He had seen them on Arlington Court. What he was looking at right now were the unmistakable impressions of Mrs. Cornblossom's sturdy walking shoes.

He put his hand on the knob of the cellar door. It turned and the door opened, just a crack. Inside, all was darkness. He was confused and uncertain. No one had seen Mrs. Cornblossom for months. Why would she be walking about up here this morning? How would she even get here?

And then, as he opened the door another fraction of an inch, he heard a voice. It was not a human voice at all—not even a sound that anyone else could have heard. And yet there was a message, a clear message with intelligence and significance, in this tingling that came from somewhere in the center of his body. And he knew: this was what was it must have felt like in the old days, when people were able to understand the animals.

The voice, kind but firm, told him, "The time has not come."

Gently, Caleb closed the door. He ran to catch up

with Ed. He did not mention the voice, nor the sense of mystery and fear and wonder that was upon him all the way back to Arlington Court.

CHAPTER SEVEN:
NELL'S DIARY

It was the first morning of a new year and the middle of a snowy winter. Outside the windows of Arlington Court, snow on snow filled the courtyard with silence, turning sidewalks and gardens and bushes into a single, lumpy blanket of white. No footprints or paw prints crossed it yet, not even those of the cat Cocobean. Inside her house, Nell opened the first page of her new diary. The page was as blank and white as the snow-covered sidewalk.

Nell was still wearing her flannel pajamas, and her hair was a mass of dark tangles. Curled on the sofa beside her Teddy bear, she chewed at her thumb and wondered how to begin.

The diary was a birthday present from her father. Nell didn't like having her birthday at the end of December. It wasn't fair that the most special day of her year happened to be when everyone else had had more than enough of holidays, parties, and singing. It meant that her birthday was likely to be overlooked, or at least celebrated without much fuss. And it meant, as she already had discovered, that people gave her calendars and diaries and other things that had been marked down to half-price after the holiday shopping season.

It hadn't really been an awful day, she had to admit. Of course, this was a special year. Nell was ten now. Her age required two numbers instead of a single one. She would be in double digits, as Caleb had pointed out, until she was a hundred years old, and she might die before she reached a hundred. Her father had taken her out for dinner and allowed her to order from the adult menu, and had not complained when she finished less than a third of her spaghetti dinner.   Afterwards they went back to Arlington Court, where Inchbald had prepared a surprise party with cookies and ice cream. It was a nice thing for him to do, even if the cookies, which were shaped like pine trees and candy canes, were obviously leftovers from an earlier party. Caleb and Ed had popped up from behind the sofa, calling out "Surprise! Happy birthday!"

She was surprised, but somehow it wasn't perfect. It seemed to Nell that she should be the happiest girl on earth, but she was not. Something was wrong with being ten.

And it wasn't just her age. For at least a month, maybe more, Nell had felt that something was changing between herself and her friends. Caleb and Ed were drawing away from her, and she felt herself feeling distant from them. It was very hard to think about, much less explain to anyone else.

Oh, they still did things together—but not as often as before. Caleb and Ed seemed to have found new interests that Nell didn't share or understand. Cars, for instance. Dinosaurs were one thing. Cars were, well, boring. And the way they talked about them. Makes and models and engines and horsepower. It made her feel left out and lonely, and she had a strange feeling that it was meant to do that.

She didn't know why they would want to exclude her.

She was the best mathematician of the three, and she could keep up with them in sports. But something was amiss. She didn't quite know what it was, but she knew it had something to do with their being boys and her being a girl.

Then, there was the matter of her own changes. Nell didn't understand this either, but she couldn't help noticing that she had a new habit. She had started to keep secrets.

For instance, there were the secret bunnies.

Just a few blocks from Arlington Court, halfway down the steep bank of the town's river, a sidewalk followed the river for several miles. Nell often rode her bicycle here, and she especially loved to ride in the early morning. She pumped the pedals with all her strength, until she almost seemed to be flying as she sped along the sidewalk. Ducks quacked and launched themselves into the river, and sparrows pitched themselves over the banks into thickets near the water. Doves made wild giggling sounds as they flew out of her path, and crows scolded her from the crab apple trees that lined the sidewalk. Once a great blue heron had played a game with her, lifting off from the bank and landing just ahead of her, again and again. She had seen mice and groundhogs and several turtles. But the rabbits were her favorites. There were rabbits almost every morning, so many that she began to count them.

One morning she surprised seventeen rabbits. When she got home, she told her father. The next day he asked, "What's the bunny count today?"

That was how it started, and Nell had been reporting the bunny count for almost as long as she had been riding her bicycle along the riverbank. It was an actual tradition, which somehow made it twice as bad when, for no reason she could think of, she began to lie. Well, perhaps it wasn't really lying. She never told her father that there were more bunnies than she had seen. If she saw six rabbits on a certain morning, she might say that she had seen only five. After all, Nell told herself, if you see six rabbits, you must have seen five rabbits. She was merely keeping a bunny or two all to herself.

And—this was something else she could not explain—she needed that secret bunny. She just had to have that one bunny.

She had another secret, too. Although Nell and Caleb and Ed had shared books for years, she somehow could not bring herself to tell them what she had been reading lately: poetry. During October, at school, the teacher had read a poem about autumn. The poem described Nell's feeling about autumn perfectly. Sometimes the trees and sky were so full of beauty that Nell thought she would break into pieces, or melt into a puddle, if one more lovely thing were added to what was already there. It amazed and gladdened her to discover that someone else had felt just the same way. She asked to borrow the book, and copied it word for word:

> O World, I cannot hold thee close enough!
>   Thy winds, thy wide grey skies!
>   Thy mists that roll and rise!
> Thy woods, this autumn day, that ache and sag
> And all but cry with colour! That gaunt crag
> To crush! To lift the lean of that black bluff!
> World, World, I cannot get thee close enough!
>
> Long have I known a glory in it all,
>   But never knew I this;
>   Here such a passion is
> As stretcheth me apart. Lord, I do fear
> Thou'st made the world too beautiful this year.

My soul is all but out of me,—let fall
No burning leaf; prithee, let no bird call.

The poet's name was Edna St. Vincent Millay, and the poem was called "God's World." Nell had heard this name before, from Mrs. Cornblossom, whose name was also Edna. In fact, Nell was probably one of the few people on earth who knew that Mrs. Cornblossom had been named after Edna Millay.

"Oh, many girls were given that name," she had told Nell. "You see, for my generation, Edna Millay was like a rock star or a fashion model. Back then, if you can imagine, they didn't have rock music or fashion magazines. But people went wild over poets." Mrs. Cornblossom had even given Nell a book of Edna Millay's poems, saying she might enjoy them when she was a little older.

She did, although perhaps "enjoy" wasn't the word for how the poems made Nell feel. Some of them were sad, and they made her cry. Some of them she couldn't understand at all. Her favorites were about birds and flowers and trees. She had thought about showing Toothbucket a poem that was made of nothing but tree words, because she knew he would like that. But she didn't think he would care for the others. And she was certain that Caleb and Ed would make fun of her if they knew.

Nell wished she could talk with Mrs. Cornblossom about how lonely she felt these days. She thought Mrs. Cornblossom would understand about even the secret bunnies.

She turned the diary over in her hands. This wasn't what she wanted for her birthday. She had asked for the only thing she wanted more than anything in the world, a kitten. Her father had told her a long time ago that when she was about ten, she would be old enough to take care of a pet. And she had made it a point to remind him of that as her birthday drew near. In fact, she had reminded him so many times that one morning he was cross, and told her, "Don't wear that wish out, Nell."

She guessed she had worn out the wish, because her birthday came and went, and there was no kitten. But she hadn't stopped wishing it. She simply wasn't talking about it anymore. She still wanted a kitten, wanted it so much that she could feel her insides get all tangled and tense when she imagined what it would be like to have a little cat snuggling beside her in bed, or purring in her lap while she read, or playing with a ball of yarn, or drinking milk from a saucer in the kitchen.

The diary was really just a blank book. It didn't even have a lock and key, the way some diaries do. It was bound in red handmade paper from Japan. Sprays of pink blossoms were scattered across the cover, along with what looked like multicolored balls of yarn (this made her think of a kitten again), and the paper had a plush feel that was good to touch. Inside were a hundred and sixty-eight pages—she had counted them—which would last her for almost a year, if she wrote on both sides of each page, one side a day.

It was her private book, her father had said. There was no need for a lock and key. "I will not read it," he told her, "even if you leave it lying on the living room floor. You are your own person, and you should have a place for your private thoughts."

How to begin? It didn't feel comfortable to write, "Dear Diary." If nobody, including her father, was going to read it, who was this "dear" person? On the other hand, it didn't feel right to address her thoughts to nobody. The one person to whom she felt close was Edna St. Vincent Millay, but Mrs. Cornblossom had told her that Edna Millay was dead, and what was the point of writing a letter to someone who was dead?

Then it came to her. She would write to Mrs. Cornblossom. She didn't know for sure where Mrs. Cornblossom was, or whether she would ever come back to Arlington Court. But, if she did, she would want to know what had happened while she was gone. Nell was sure of that. And Nell knew that things get forgotten unless you write them down. Also, Mrs. Cornblossom probably wouldn't mind if Nell called her "Edna." It would be almost like writing to Edna St. Vincent Millay.

That was settled, then. Nell licked the end of her pencil. "Dear Edna," she wrote. "My father has broken my heart."

She told about the kitten, and then about the secret bunnies. She told about the way Caleb and Ed were acting. She began to feel better. Or rather, she forgot about how bad she felt. She forgot that she had meant to use only one side of a page each day, and filled page after page. She forgot where she was.

Best of all, she forgot who she was. After she had told Dear Edna everything she could tell, a very strange thing happened. As if it had a mind of its own, the pencil in her hand moved to the next page. To her astonishment, Nell watched it write, "Dear Nell." And then, underneath that, "I am very happy to hear from you. Now, this is important, so pay attention: Your father isn't really a bad person, he simply doesn't understand. Try not to hate him, dear."

At the bottom of the page, in her best cursive, Nell wrote, "Love, Edna."

When her father came downstairs, she didn't even notice him until he brought a cup of hot cocoa into the living room and said, "Happy New Year, Honey." Nell shut the diary, jumped up from the couch, and hugged him hard.

CHAPTER EIGHT:
THE VALENTINE

Every year, there comes a day in February when the sun, which has been keeping itself wrapped in clouds and low in the sky, ventures out to see if the world has missed it. The clouds turn from wool to cotton to silk chiffon, and the sun smiles through them. Like a patient recovering from a long illness, it is shy and a bit wobbly, but so glad to be greeting its neighbors—mountains and valleys, trees and moss.

Streams and rivers sparkle like gold embroidery threads in a crazy quilt. Clumps of moss grow plump and plush. In their burrows, small animals shift, stretch, and yawn. Before they go back to sleep, they breathe in a faint but wonderful smell, a complicated perfume made of melting snow, wet soil, roots, and worms. This is the time of winter when animals dream their most delicious and fragile dreams. In their dreams, beavers dance jigs to the rhythms of water tumbling over creek beds, and slap their tails in time. Rabbits dream of flying, and of their fur ruffling in silver spangles under a full moon.

Like the sun, Toothbucket was growing stronger every day. His friend Inchbald had nursed him for more than a month. At least three times a week, Inchbald carried a large thermos bottle from his house to Toothbucket's house. In it was soup—sometimes chicken soup with carrots and noodles and sometimes split pea soup with bits of ham —that had simmered for hours on the stovetop. Inchbald poured the steaming soup into a blue ceramic mug and took it upstairs to the bedroom, where Toothbucket lay surrounded by books, a hot water bottle, tissues, and cough medicines. The cat Cocobean was always there, too, curled like a miniature braided rug at the foot of the bed.

"I say, Toothbucket, you look almost like yourself today," Inchbald announced on this morning. He set the soup on a tray next to the bed. "You've come around, haven't you? Indeed, it will be no surprise to see you go marching off into the wilderness again before the week is out, challenging the elements without a proper hat or muffler. Ah, my dear Toothbucket, whatever shall we do with you?"

Toothbucket's long face formed itself into a wreath of happy wrinkles. In the recent weeks, he had thanked Inchbald so many times that it was no longer necessary to say it aloud. The accident of his illness and Inchbald's care for him had made the two of them more than neighbors. When Toothbucket was fidgeting and moaning with fever, Inchbald had stationed himself at the bedside with a damp washcloth to cool the sick man's forehead. When Toothbucket coughed so deeply that it seemed his lungs would turn inside out, Inchbald had rubbed his friend's sore chest with menthol and oil and wrapped warm towels around his neck. Near the bed, Inchbald had installed a vaporizer that bubbled and murmured companionably as it exhaled a comforting mist.

No one, not even Mrs. Cornblossom, could have been a better nurse. And yet, when this occurred to Toothbucket, he felt guilty for thinking it, and his eyes suddenly overflowed with tears. He sneezed, sending tissues flying and sheets flapping around him.

"No, you won't be trekking across the frozen tundra this day," Inchbald said. "But you are mending nicely, and it's uncommonly pleasant outside. I daresay a bit of fresh air and sunshine would do you good. What would you say to a short spell in the rocking chair on your front porch? In about forty-eight minutes, by my calculation, the sun will reach across the courtyard and cast a beam in just the right spot."

Toothbucket took a deep breath. For the first time in weeks, it didn't hurt. "That would be wonderful," he said slowly.

"You will, of course, want to dress warmly, and perhaps wrap yourself in a quilt."

"Of course," Toothbucket agreed, and gave a solemn nod.

"And wear two pairs of socks," Inchbald said sternly.

It took almost forty-five minutes for Toothbucket to get dressed. Each small procedure of every ordinary task was elaborate, unfamiliar, and full of delight. He held up his favorite flannel shirt, which Inchbald had laundered and folded neatly in the second drawer of the bureau. It felt to his fingertips like the deepest velvet. When he buckled his overalls, he marvelled at the satisfying weight of the brass loops and buttons, and admired the way they were burnished by wear. He noticed that the hole in the right leg of his overalls had been expertly mended.

His knees felt as if they had turned to rubber, but when he stooped to pull on the first of the two pairs of socks, his spine creaked like a bicycle chain left out in the weather to rust. And when he peered into the cracked bathroom mirror, he hardly recognized himself. His reflected face was thinner than the one he remembered, and his beard had twisted itself into a sort of corkscrew that pointed off to one side.

Holding the handrail, Toothbucket stepped cautiously down the stairway to the first floor. His house, too, was almost unrecognizable. But if his beard had gone awry, his house was transformed in another way. A few motes of dust danced in the air where the sun came slanting through the front window, but the soft whorls of spiders' webs and cat hair that usually gathered in the corners were missing. His old rag rugs looked fluffy and fresh, as if they had been shaken and aired, and each one lay in perfect alignment with the walls. Beneath them, the wooden floors gleamed.

In the kitchen, his few pots and pans hung in neat succession, from small to large, on their hooks. The sink was empty and the dishes stacked in the cupboard. His copper kettle had been polished to a fine glow.

As Inchbald had suggested, Toothbucket decided to take a quilt out to the porch with him. He lifted his wool crazy quilt from its place on the back of the worn sofa in the front room. Toothbucket's own grandmother had made the quilt, and he treasured it above almost any other thing. Its surface was a jumble of different shapes, colors and patterns; and the dark red embroidery that joined the pieces was a museum of stitchery. Toothbucket's grandmother had once told him the names of all the stitches, but he couldn't remember any of them, so he had made up his own names. One he called the chicken-pecking stitch. Another was the trillium stitch, for its meandering path left a trail of tiny trefoils that made him think of the trillium bloom. One stitch resembled pampas grass, and another reminded him of nothing so much as the droppings of deer.

Toothbucket settled himself on the porch. His rocking chair made its creaky music. Cocobean darted through the cat door and jumped into his lap. The sun made him squint, but it felt fine on his face. He closed his eyes. For a few minutes, he must have slept. He dreamed that he was a child again, not older than eight years, and that he was helping his grandmother hang clean sheets on the clothesline, the sun and whiteness dazzling and dizzying him.

"Toothbucket!"

He awoke with a snort. Had he dreamed a child's voice calling his name? Or was it his own, eight-year-old self calling to him across the years?

The voice belonged to Nell, the little girl who lived on the other side of the court. She stood beside his rocking chair. Her eyes were level with his own.

"Toothbucket, do you know what day it is?"

"I don't," he admitted. "My goodness, Nell, I don't even know what day of the week it is."

"It's Tuesday. And, Toothbucket, it's Valentine's Day!"

"That would make it the fourteenth of February," Toothbucket said.

"Right. Have you looked in your mailbox today?"

"Why, no, I haven't. I think Inchbald has been bringing in my mail lately."

"Well, I thought I saw the postman leave you something today. Has Inchbald brought your mail in today?"

"I don't know." Toothbucket scooted his rocking chair over toward the mailbox that hung next to his door. Still seated, he lifted the lid and stuck his hand down into the box. At first it felt empty, but then his fingers bumped against a small something in the corner. He took it out. It was a greeting card made of red construction paper in the shape of a heart. A heart-shaped paper doily was glued to the front. There was no envelope and no stamp.

"I thought so," said Nell. Then she skipped down the stairs. "See you later, Toothbucket," she called as she ran up the steps to her own house. "I'm glad you're feeling better."

The greeting was written in a careful cursive. It consisted of four lines that made a short poem.

> *I ask a friend to write this*
> *For another friend I know*
> *To tell him that I miss him*
> *And that I love him so.*

Underneath the poem, in the same rounded penmanship, was a name: Edna.

The daylight was failing when Toothbucket climbed the stairs in his house again. A clean towel was draped over his shoulder. In his unusually tidy bathroom, he ran hot water until the bathtub was full and the mirror clouded with steam. He eased himself in and let the warmth soak into every pore. It seemed to him that nothing had ever felt so good. He scrubbed himself until his lanky old body tingled, and then he lathered his hair and beard and tugged a comb through both soapy masses of hair.

Finally he lowered his head so that the water from the tap would run directly over it, and turned on the water again. As warm water flowed over Toothbucket's head, he began to sing. He made up the words to the song as he felt them, and they told of redemption and boundless joy and love that cannot be lost or diminished. Then there were no more words, only a melody that rolled and dipped and swelled. His voice and the water together made a wild warbling sound not unlike the call of a loon on a northern lake.

CHAPTER NINE:
COCOBEAN'S ADVENTURE

Cocobean the cat had been born on Arlington Court and had lived all her life there. A world that is only one block long and three stories high is not large enough for most children, but it is quite adequate for most cats.

Inside the house she shared with Toothbucket, besides all the floors and chairs and couches she could sit upon, were many places to which a lively cat could leap with no trouble. Toothbucket's shelves and tabletops were filled with interesting objects: photographs of old people in stiff, starched collars; buttons and marbles and foreign coins, books that smelled of dust and mold; a Japanese fan, half-open, with sprays of white blossoms tucked into every fold; an old and much-used pocket knife. One shelf held a collection of dried seed pods in various forms, including a lotus pod that made a delightful skittering noise and performed a bouncy, unpredictable dance when batted by a paw.

On this early spring day, however, Cocobean was too restless to stay indoors. She ran through the cat door to the outside. The frosty morning had given way to an afternoon of delicious smells and joyous discoveries. The first daffodils of the year, like small cornucopias of sunlight, had already bloomed in Toothbucket's garden.

Icy patches on the sidewalk turned to slush, then to puddles. Birds announced that they had arrived to stay for the season and greeted one another with excited twitters.

Cocobean wandered from one yard to another, looking at everything. She dipped one paw into a large puddle and watched rings of light spread outward in circles. Then she shook her paw and licked it. She meandered between the blade-like leaves of daffodils that had not yet shown their petals, nosing the tight buds as if to spread the news that it was time to bloom. She climbed up the trunk of the pawpaw tree to get a good view of the courtyard, then raced down to inspect some small source of movement, perhaps a mouse scurrying between two empty flowerpots on Inchbald's porch.

Now something even more enticing captured her attention. At the far end of the court, just beyond the gate, a brilliant cardinal darted into an unkempt patch of forsythia. For a long time, the cat sat watching, her face turning this way and that as she followed the movements of the redbird.

Then she saw another bird, a robin. It flew toward a large holly tree, trailing a piece of string. As she watched, another bird came. This one carried a length of glittery tinsel that must have fallen from someone's Christmas tree. It, too, disappeared into the dark foliage. They were building a nest.

Cocobean had never desired to venture past either of the two wrought-iron gates, one at each end of the sidewalk, that enclosed the neighborhood. Perhaps she did not really want to do it now, even as she slipped between two of the iron bars. She put one paw on the other side, then another. She stood that way, half in and half out, for a long minute, her eyes darting back and forth with the birds, her tail twitching like a metronome.

Then she slid forward, into the big world outside Arlington Court.

She went to the base of the holly tree and looked up, trying to catch sight of a flash of feather among the glossy leaves, but the birds were well hidden.

She walked along the sidewalk until it ended at another sidewalk that led in a different direction. Crossing it, she came to a strip of grass, just like the grass in Arlington Court. Beyond that was a single step and yet another sidewalk, except that this one was much, much wider.

Cocobean stopped. She wondered what beings walked on this path. Might they be giants, with legs as big as trees, their heads so high in the air that they could look into an attic window? Might they wear sweaters as large as Toothbucket's quilt?

Even as she stood pondering, a monster appeared. Cocobean saw it careening toward her from around a corner. It made a growling noise and its enormous eyes shone like huge light bulbs. Its mouth was a wide, shining thing, and it was coming toward her at such a terrible speed that she had no hope of escaping. Cocobean stood frozen, unable to move.

The monster let out three ear-splitting blasts of sound, louder by far than all of Inchbald's clocks chiming together. The noise vibrated all the way to tip of her tail. The beast was upon her. Its great teeth reflected the sunlight. Still she could not move.

The monster made an awful shrieking, screeching noise. It veered this way and that, and came to a halt just inches from where Cocobean cowered. The heat from its huge body rolled toward her in a sickening wave, along with a smell of something burning. She waited for it to snatch her and crush her between its gleaming teeth.

To her surprise, it did not even touch her. Instead,

growling only slightly, it slowly glided away.

Cocobean found that she could move again, although her legs felt limp and uncertain. She backed away from the wide monster pathway, then turned quickly and made for Arlington Court. She could hardly wait to be safe on her own porch—or, better yet, napping on Toothbucket's bed.

Then she saw the dog. It lay in a black-and-white heap in the middle of the walkway that led to her home. The dog lifted its massive head and looked directly at her. Cocobean's back arched. Her fur stood on end.

The dog got to its feet, shook its shaggy body, and came toward her. It began to bark.

In that moment, Cocobean forgot about the beast that had nearly crushed her. She forgot about the porch, and the bed, and Toothbucket. She forgot about home and comfort. She remembered only one thing. She remembered how to run. She dashed away from the dog. Without even knowing it, she streaked all the way across the wide path where she had nearly met her destruction. She ran as fast as she had ever run, paying no attention to where she was going. She came to another avenue for monsters and crossed it. Then another. She didn't stop to see if the dog was getting closer or listen to hear if its barking was louder. She ran until she could run no more.

When she stopped, she saw that she was beside another of the huge pathways, and that another beast, this time a bright red one, was approaching. But Cocobean was too exhausted to care.

Like the first monster, this one glided past her. As it did, Cocobean was met with a horrible sight. She could see into the upper part of the monster. In its belly were two live people, tied up with ropes. The monster had swallowed them whole. They stared straight ahead and did not even try to escape.

From this monster, as it passed, came a deep, insistent thumping and the sound of a man's angry voice shouting in rhythm with the beat. Cocobean couldn't make out the words, but she understood that the monster spoke human language. The beast must be threatening its victims.

Yet another monster glided past. It, too, paid no attention to Cocobean. But it also held people—a woman and two small boys. One of them was crying.

More of the monsters came and went. People were trapped in all of them. Some of the beasts were going in one direction and some in the other. None of them seemed to notice Cocobean. Perhaps these ogres devoured only humans. Perhaps they didn't like the taste of cats.

Cocobean saw that she was in a high place. Beside her was a railing, not unlike the gate at Arlington Court, but one that stretched on and on. On the other side of this one, however, there was nothing but air. She stepped closer and put out her paw to test it. She peered over the edge.

Far below her, something like a ribbon glimmered. It looked very much like the stream of water that trickled out of the hose and across the yard when Toothbucket watered his garden. It must be water. And this place, where she was—where the great, growling creatures passed back and forth with their bellies full of humans— this must be a way to cross over the water.

Cocobean stood still and tried to think. Should she go forward? What dangers lay ahead, she could not imagine. But she knew what was behind her—the dog. She could no longer hear barking, only the sounds of the gliding beasts. But the dog might be waiting. Besides, she had no idea where she was or how to find her way home.

Ahead of her, on the other side of the stream of water, she could see a hillside with trees. She made up her mind. Moving slowly and stopping often to look and listen for danger, Cocobean went forward.

The path sloped downward to a place where the large beasts separated and went in several different directions. But there was a smaller pathway, also, much too narrow for the creatures to navigate. She followed it. It led along a stone wall draped with ivy. Compared to the beasts' road, the dirt beneath her paws felt cool and soft. The growling noises faded, and she began to hear other, familiar sounds: the twitters of birds and the rustle of leaves as a gust of wind blew through the trees.

She came to an opening in the wall. On the other side, she saw, the path continued, shaded by tall hemlock trees. She ventured inside the walled place, stopped, and listened intently. She couldn't hear anything frightening.

And there were good smells here: daffodil, magnolia, and wild onion. Small blue flowers grew beside the path, and Cocobean recognized them. This same sort of flower grew in Toothbucket's garden, all along the edges. Encouraged, she walked further. The trail wound back and forth several times, always going upward.

She kept going until she saw, ahead of her, a very large house. But there were no lights inside, and she noticed that one of the upper windows was broken. As she stared, a black shape came dancing out of it. It dipped and whirled prettily in the twilight.

It was growing dark, Cocobean realized. It was the time of day when bats come out to look for their dinners, and when good little cats sit with their human companions on porches.

The darkness settled in. Mist enveloped the shadows. Something rustled in the ivy. From somewhere above, an owl called, "Who? Who?" It was not a friendly greeting.

Then, quite close to Cocobean, there was a flapping of wings, a scuffling sound, and a small, piercing cry that ended abruptly. The owl had found its dinner.

But there was to be no dinner for Cocobean. Would she ever again share a can of tuna fish with Toothbucket? Would she ever again sit in his lap and feel his rough old hand petting her? Would she ever drink cream from a porcelain saucer in Inchbald's dining room? Would she ever see any of her friends again?

For the first time since the beginning of her adventure, Cocobean cried. She wailed. She howled to the hemlocks and the hillside. She filled the velvet night with her misery.

And someone spoke to her.

"Cocobean," the voice said, "is that you?"

Cocobean stopped crying. This was a voice she knew and trusted. Not Toothbucket's voice. Not Inchbald's voice. It was the soft, comforting, slightly crackly voice of an old woman.

"There's no need to be afraid now," the voice said reassuringly, and a shape stepped from behind the trunk of a large beech tree. Cocobean was too astonished to make even a squeak.

"Yes, it must surprise you," said Mrs. Cornblossom, "to see that I am a cat."

CHAPTER TEN:
THE REUNION

Inchbald was barely out of bed, still wearing his favorite nightshirt and floppy-bunny slippers, savoring the first sip of his first cup of tea, when a thunderous pounding at the front door interrupted his morning ritual.

"Whatever is the matter?" he said, a trifle crossly, when he saw Toothbucket standing on the porch. But then he saw a tear forming in Toothbucket's left eye.

"It's Cocobean," Toothbucket said, and now the tear welled up, tipped over the edge, and rolled down the already damp landscape of his long, craggy face. "She's missing. She was gone all night. Is she here?"

"No—and she didn't visit me yesterday. As a matter of fact, I thought that a bit odd. She has taken to coming by nearly every day, you know, to see if a bit of cream has appeared in a bowl, very mysteriously, in the corner of the dining room." Inchbald chuckled a bit.

Toothbucket heaved a great sigh. "I haven't seen her since yesterday morning. She likes to go out by herself very early, while I am still dozing. That's the last time I saw her.

"I put food in her bowl, but none of it has been eaten. I reckoned she was turning up her nose. She does that sometimes. Then I thought she might have been visiting you. But I was distracted by my garden plans, and I just didn't bother to look for her until—until late. Then I looked in all of her favorite places. Sometimes she goes under the stairway in the basement. And she likes to sit on the braided rug up in the attic. If she's not in one place, she's nearly always in the other."

"Dear old Toothbucket," Inchbald said kindly. "Don't cats do this? Surely she will be back soon."

Toothbucket gave a loud hiccup, and his voice broke. "She's never been gone all night," he moaned.

Inchbald looked around the porch, as if the naughty cat might be lurking behind one of his flowerpots. Then, because he could think of nothing else to say, he asked, "Would you like a cup of tea?"

"I ought to have come last night," Toothbucket continued. "I didn't begin to worry in earnest until late in the evening, and then your lights were out."

"Yes, I went to bed quite early. I wanted to be well refreshed for a full day of cookery. You do remember about our dinner party, don't you? You promised to contribute a rare delicacy, if you recall."

Toothbucket had forgotten. He had promised to bring Inchbald a mess of ramps, those rich and earthy wild onions that grow only in special places during early spring. But now he could think of nothing but Cocobean. Instead of answering his friend's question, he only nodded his head slowly as he turned and walked back down the steps.

"I say, Toothbucket," Inchbald called after him, "if there is anything I can do to help, I shall be only too delighted." But Toothbucket seemed not to hear him.

As Toothbucket trudged back to his own house, young Nell came out on her front porch.

"Have you seen Cocobean?" he said. He repeated his

sad story. But Nell had not seen Cocobean. Nobody had seen Cocobean for a whole day.

For what seemed like the hundredth time, Toothbucket trudged up to the attic and looked at the braided rug, as if he could make the cat appear there simply by concentrating on the empty spot where he wished to see her—exactly the way the cat stared at her empty food bowl when she wished it to be filled. Then he went down to the basement, this time with a flashlight, to look in the dusty crawl space underneath the stairs. But the flashlight beam showed only a few cobwebs and the dry husk of a hickory nut.

There was simply no denying it: Cocobean had disappeared. She has gone the way Mrs. Cornblossom did, Toothbucket thought to himself. One day the world is orderly and sensible. Then, without warning, someone necessary and dear simply vanishes, and nothing is ever the same. You go on. You have to. But the empty space stays, and nothing ever fills it.

Perhaps, Toothbucket thought, this is how it will be for me. My world will become nothing but empty spaces. First Mrs. Cornblossom, then the sarvis tree. Now Cocobean is missing. Will Inchbald be next? And what if everything and everyone I love is taken away, one by one? How will I know who I am? Will I even exist?

By late morning, Toothbucket had become so anxious that the house simply couldn't contain him. Once more, he went to see Inchbald. Again his neighbor invited him to sit and drink a cup of tea, but Toothbucket paced back and forth in the dining room, rattling the china in the cupboards and combing his bony hands through his long beard.

The clocks chimed the noon hour. Inchbald pulled out his pocket watch to confirm the time.

"Perhaps," he said gently, "we ought to postpone our

dinner party. I daresay you are not in the mood for a social event, Toothbucket."

Toothbucket stopped pacing and looked down at his friend. "No," he said sadly. "I'm not in the mood. But it would be worse to be alone, and to have nothing at all to do. Please go on with the dinner party, Inchbald. I will go dig those ramps now."

"It will give you something to occupy yourself," Inchbald said.

"You go on," Toothbucket said aloud, still trying to convince himself that he would, in fact, go on. "You have to."

"That's the spirit," Inchbald agreed. "I'll make you a sandwich to carry with you. It wouldn't surprise me at all to learn that you have neglected to eat breakfast."

And so, with his old knife in his pocket, a brown paper sandwich bag in his hand, and a large canvas sack hanging from his shoulder, Toothbucket set off for the patch of ramps that grew beside the abandoned mansion. His head drooped mournfully, and he walked more slowly than usual. He hardly noticed the warmth of the sun or the various fragrances of the spring breeze, which played this way and that about him. Still, walking outdoors was better than pacing indoors. And he had to admit that Inchbald was right: It was good to have something to do.

He crossed the bridge, rounded the corner of the stone wall, and ducked his head to go under the archway. From beside the path, bluets winked up at him. They reminded him of Mrs. Cornblossom's eyes.

A little further along on the trail, trilliums nodded their triangular heads, and Virginia bluebells dangled from their stems. Further still, in the same place where it sprang up each year, a jack-in-the-pulpit stood at attention. Toothbucket noticed these things, but they did not cheer him in the ordinary way of spring.

At the top of the hill, the broken sarvis tree still lay across the stone bench where it had fallen, its dead branches unadorned by white blossoms. Toothbucket saw that the bench was cracked, too. Someday even the mansion would crumble and go to pieces, and nothing would be left but a heap of rubble. Later still, moss and leaves would cover them all. Toothbucket sighed and placed his sandwich bag on the corner of the cracked bench.

Ramps were springing up all over the hillside. To a passerby, their broad leaves might have resembled lily of the valley, but their savory smell was very different from that plant's crisp perfume. Toothbucket thrust his knife blade into the moist soil and cut the bulb at its base, taking care to leave the root of the plant buried so that it would spring up again next year. He brought the white bulb to his nose and inhaled deeply. The delicious, earthy smell seemed to anticipate all of its usual accompaniments—fried potatoes, fresh eggs, maybe even a frothy mug of Inchbald's dark, home-brewed beer. But when he thought about the supper Inchbald would prepare tonight, Toothbucket could only think of it as the second evening without Cocobean. A tear splashed on the leaf of the ramp. Toothbucket sighed and continued with his task.

He moved about the hillside, choosing and digging, sometimes sitting down to arrange ramps into neat bundles, which he tied together with lengths of string before stowing them in his bag. Finally he had collected enough ramps to fill the canvas sack. Inchbald would be pleased.

Toothbucket wiped his knife against one leg of his overalls, removing most of the mud and soil. He folded the blade in and put the knife into his back pocket. Then he remembered his sandwich, and realized that, despite his heavy heart, he was feeling hungry. But his hands were as muddy as the knife had been. He brushed them against the legs of his trousers. Then he remembered that there was a well with a water pump on the other side of the old mansion. He wasn't sure if the pump still worked, but it was worth trying.

He climbed the hill and walked around the perimeter of the mansion, following the path that bordered the long-abandoned kitchen garden. The pump stood a few feet from the house, near a small stairway that led down to a cellar door, which hung slightly ajar. If he had been in a better mood, and if he had brought his flashlight, Toothbucket might have inspected that dim cellar, just to see what there was to see. But today was not the day for exploring.

He pulled and pushed the pump handle. At first there was nothing but squeaking—a loud complaint, as if the old machine were trying to tell him it had worked hard for a long time and now wished to be left in peace. But soon a trickle of water came from the spout, and then a gush. Toothbucket gave an extra few pushes on the handle, then plunged his hands under the cold water, rubbing them together to loosen the caked mud. He lowered his head sideways, let the water spill into his mouth, tipped back his head, and made a satisfying gargling noise.

From below and behind came an answering noise. Not a gargle, but a meow. No, not merely a meow, but the amazing, the one-and-only, the inimitable, beloved voice of his lost Cocobean. Toothbucket swivelled his head, sputtered, and spit out water. Cocobean was peeking around the edge of the cellar door!

He knelt at the top of the stairway. "Cocobean!" he whispered. "Cocobean, can it be you?" For reply, the little cat scampered into his arms and rubbed her head against the bib of his overalls.

For a time they sat together on the top step. Toothbucket laughed aloud and cried a little, too, with relief, all the while caressing the little cat, who purred ardently and frequently tipped her head back to gaze at Toothbucket with wide, amber eyes.

After a while, though, Toothbucket roused himself. "We must go home and tell Inchbald," he said. "And, of course, I must bring home the ramps. Oh, Cocobean, what a beautiful day this is. What a wonderful day!" With the cat nestled against his chest, he managed to hoist the heavy canvas sack to his shoulder. He made his way toward the stone bench. He would eat his sandwich on the way home, he decided. He would share it with Cocobean.

But as he stooped to pick up the sandwich bag, the cat bounded away. Toothbucket dropped his sack and ran after her, scolding, "Cocobean! Come back!"

She sprinted toward the cellar door, ran down the stairway, and stood at the bottom, looking up at him.

"Cocobean, come along. This is no time for a game," Toothbucket pleaded. He bent down again and coaxed the cat with his open hand.

"Don't you want to go home?" he said.

Cocobean edged backwards, curling herself around the door. She slipped inside.

"Cocobean!" cried Toothbucket. He went down the short stairway. He pulled the heavy door open far enough to enter. In the dimness, he heard a small sound from the other side of the dank cellar.

He went forward inch by inch in the darkness, bowing his head to avoid bumping against the low ceiling. Cocobean purred, calling him on.

Slowly, Toothbucket's eyes became accustomed

to the dark. Following his cat's voice, he moved slowly to the far corner of the cellar. There, on a pile of rags, illuminated by a shaft of light from a hole where some bricks were missing from the wall, lay another cat. Its grey coat was matted and filthy. Both of the cat's front paws were a tawny white, as if it wore wool stockings. It lifted its head and looked at Toothbucket with serene eyes that were a startling light blue color. Toothbucket felt a jolt of something like recognition.

Between the cat's front and back paws, tucked safely within the circle of their mother's body, were two sleeping kittens.

CHAPTER ELEVEN:
THE PARTY

"Tell me again how you carried them all back," Nell said. She sat at one end of Toothbucket's couch with the two kittens nestled in her lap. At the other end, Cocobean was curled into a ball, also fast asleep. The smell of a recent banquet of canned tuna fish still lingered.

Toothbucket sat on the floor, brushing the fur of the mother cat, who looked much lovelier than she had a few hours before. After feeding both hungry cats, Toothbucket had given her a thorough bath—which, amazingly, she did not seem to mind—wrapped her in a towel, and brought her downstairs.

He had carefully combed every burr and tangle from the cat's fur. Now it was dry and soft, but he continued to brush her because she seemed to enjoy it so. She purred continuously, stopping only occasionally to lick one of her white paws or to gaze upward at Nell and the kittens.

"It wasn't a chore," Toothbucket replied. "I found an empty wooden box there in the cellar, so I put Mama Cat and her babies into it and carried them home. With a bag of ramps slung across one shoulder," he added.

"And Cocobean rode on your other shoulder?"

"All the way," Toothbucket said, with a fond glance at his sleeping cat.

Nell turned her attention back to the kittens. One was solid grey, a shade lighter than its mother. The other was also grey, but the color was mixed with streaks of darker colors. It looked a bit like the camouflage pants her friend Caleb sometimes wore. Brindle, Toothbucket had called the pattern. Nell whispered the word over and over to herself. She liked the sound of it. She liked the word "brindle" more than the other word she had learned on this same day. She wasn't sure about the sound of "ramps"—at least, not when it meant something to eat.

"Toothbucket, do you think I will like ramps?" she asked? "What do they taste like?"

"Well, I can't rightly say," Toothbucket answered after a long silence. "People compare them to onions and garlic, but that doesn't really tell you how they taste. It's like saying that orange looks like red, which is partly true, but it doesn't get to the heart of the color orange. The truth is, ramps don't taste of onions and they don't taste of garlic. They taste the way only ramps can taste."

Wrinkling her nose, Nell said, "My father loves garlic. He puts it in everything."

As he continued to brush the mother cat, Toothbucket looked about his living room. He seemed to be searching for something.

"What are you looking for?" Nell said.

Toothbucket shook his head. "I don't know," he replied. "There's something on my mind, but it's lost in fog. There's something I'm supposed to remember, but I can't remember what it is."

"Maybe you meant to do something in the garden? Is it time to plant a certain sort of seed?"

He shook his head. "No, it's not the garden."

"You don't have a car, so it can't be time to change the oil," Nell said helpfully. "And you're too old for school, so you haven't forgotten to write an important essay."

Toothbucket sighed. "I guess I'll remember later," he said, "or not."

Cocobean stretched, yawned, stretched again, and jumped down from the couch. She rubbed against Toothbucket's leg, then strolled to the front door, where she poked her head through the little cat door at the bottom. She did not go outside, but stood there for a long minute. She sniffed, and sniffed again. A fragrance, completely invisible but as warm and insistent as a beckoning hand, curled its way into the foyer and crept across the living room.

"What is that wonderful smell?" said Nell.

Toothbucket took in a deep breath and grinned broadly. "Ramps," he said. "Inchbald must be nearly ready for us." His stomach growled, and he laughed, "I am ready for ramps, too."

"I wish we could take the kittens," Nell said. She did not say what she was thinking, wishing, and hoping as hard as she could hope. If only her father could see them, fluffy and defenseless and adorable, he would surely agree to let her keep one. He wouldn't be able to say no. Not even her father could be so hard-hearted. But there was another problem. Even if he saw them, and even if he said yes, how would she choose between them?

Toothbucket wagged his head slowly from side to side. "They are so young," he said. "I don't think they are quite ready to go to parties. But I know they will be happy to curl up with their beautiful Mama Cat. Will you help me make a bed for them in the corner?"

When the bed was made, from an old blanket that Nell folded carefully to fit into a wooden box, they placed the kittens next to their mother. Immediately they began to suckle, and the mother cat purred happily as she fed them. She turned her blue eyes up toward Toothbucket.

"There's something I can almost remember," he said

again, more to himself than to Nell, "but it's no good trying too hard. Some things don't like to be thought about straightwise. Nell, my friend, shall we go to a party?"

Nell agreed that they should, but she was still looking back at the kittens as they closed the front door.

As they climbed the steps to Inchbald's house, the cooking aroma grew stronger and ever more enticing. When Inchbald opened his front door, the fragrance rolled out to meet them.

"Come in, come in, neighbors!" Inchbald cried. "Now everyone is here!"

Inchbald had put two extra leaves into his dining room table, and it extended almost from one side of the dining room to the other, requiring three lace tablecloths to cover it. He had set the table with his very best china and, because he had invited so many people, his second-best china as well. Beside each plate, a linen napkin was rolled into a silver napkin ring. Water sparkled in crystal glasses. Inchbald had burnished his spoons, knives, and forks until they glowed. And every shining surface reflected flickering light from candles that stood like sentries in tall candlesticks.

Indeed, the whole neighborhood was crowded into Inchbald's house. Friends who had not seen each other all winter hugged and chattered. In one corner, Caleb and Ed were playing a word game that involved frogs leaping from one lily pad to another. In another, Caleb's mother was telling Ed's mother about a book she had just finished reading. Nell's father was inspecting Inchbald's grandfather clock, and he seemed to be admiring the skills of the woodworker who had fashioned its cabinet.

The clocks began to chime. From walls and corners, from high and low, melodious ringing and clanging and cuckooing filled the old house, telling the six o'clock hour. Inchbald motioned for everyone to gather around the table. As the chiming faded away, everyone looked toward him.

"Friends and neighbors," Inchbald announced, "this is a very special evening. We are about to have a delicious spring feast, which is reason enough for a party. But I have invited you here at the request of someone you know and love. This dinner is, in fact, a celebration of her affection for you."

The neighbors turned to each other. They smiled, shrugged their shoulders, and held up their hands. They did not understand.

Inchbald continued. "When I moved into this house, I found a letter addressed to me. If you will take a seat, I would like to read it to you."

Except for Inchbald, everyone sat. In the glow of candlelight, they waited. The room fell quiet. Inchbald pulled a piece of paper from beneath his plate, cleared his throat, and read aloud.

"Dear Mr. Inchbald," the letter began, "after much consideration, I have decided to sell my house to you. I think you will be an excellent neighbor for my friends on Arlington Court. And I think they will be good neighbors to you.

"Toothbucket, in particular, is a person of great worth and dignity. You will find him to be kind, peaceable, and well-informed about the natural world in general and the garden in particular. He is my best friend, and I hope he will become your friend as well. You should know that Toothbucket inclines to melancholy, especially in winter. I hope you will be gentle with him when he is sad, and I fear that he is likely to be sad during the winter to come."

Everyone looked at Toothbucket, who sat at the far end of the table, opposite Inchbald. His face had gone very red, and a tear glistened on one cheek. Despite the tear, Toothbucket's face was full of joy. He said, "Mrs. Cornblossom." Inchbald nodded and continued to read.

"For the first day of spring, I hope you will plan a special dinner," Mrs. Cornblossom had written. "Invite Toothbucket and anyone else you please, and cook anything you like, but please include a fine mess of ramps on the menu. Ask Toothbucket to dig them for you. He knows where to find the best ones. And he will tell you, as I would, that a mess of ramps in spring and a taste of pawpaw fruit in the fall are the best tonics a body could have.

"I have only one more request," the letter continued. "Will you light a candle in my honor? More than anything, I would love to be with you all. But since I will not be there, it is wonderful to think that you will be with one another."

At the end of the table, Toothbucket began to chuckle. "I remembered!" he exclaimed. "At last I remembered."

"What?" Nell said.

"Today is Mrs. Cornblossom's birthday. This is her birthday party!"

A general cheer went up, and Inchbald called, "I propose a toast to Mrs. Cornblossom!" All around the table, neighbors lifted their glasses, clinked them together, and said to one another, "To Mrs. Cornblossom!"

Nell's father spoke up. "There should be gifts at a birthday party," he said.

"Indeed there should," Inchbald agreed, "but as Mrs. Cornblossom is not here to receive them...."

"Then perhaps Nell will accept from me a long overdue gift," her father finished the sentence. He turned to Nell and said, "Toothbucket tells me that there are some kittens who need a good home."

"Oh, papa," Nell cried, "may I finally have a kitten?"

"No," he said, "but you may have two kittens, as soon as they are ready to leave their mother. And Toothbucket assures me it won't be long."

Nell squealed and jumped out of her chair to hug both her father and Toothbucket. Everyone at the table applauded.

"Now," Inchbald said, "let us eat!" He lifted the top from a silver chafing dish and began to spoon out servings from a steaming heap of fried potatoes and ramps. At the other end of the table, Toothbucket ladled asparagus soup. Plates and bowls were passed from person to person. Butter melted into homemade bread, and a platter of cheeses made the round. Conversation gave way to satisfied sighs.

"Don't forget to save room for rhubarb pie," Inchbald reminded his guests. "Toothbucket told me it was Mrs. Cornblossom's specialty, and I like to imagine that I have done her proud."

Outside, the courtyard grew dark. Above the rooftops, a narrow sliver of moon brightened. One by one, stars began to wink and glitter. No one was walking through Arlington Court tonight, for every person who lived in the neighborhood was inside Inchbald's house, where the party was in progress.

On the porch next-door, a calico cat and a grey cat were curled up together on the rocking chair. From time to time, one of them raised her head and looked toward the lighted windows. And, although they did not speak in human words, they talked together quietly.

"They are eating rhubarb pie now," said the calico cat.

"Mmmm," the grey cat replied. "What a wonderful party."

THE END

ACKNOWLEDGEMENTS

Thanks to Neal Peterson, who got me started.

Many friends, too numerous to list here, have read this book or listened to parts of it, read it to their children, or helped to publish it by backing a Kickstarter.com project. I appreciate all of you.

Thanks to the children who have read or listened to this story, or parts of it, in manuscript form. Special thanks to Anise, Christian, Emma, Grace, Owen, and dozens of Mountaineer Montessori School students.

I gratefully acknowledge the Wurlitzer Foundation of Taos, New Mexico, where much of the book was written.

Edna St. Vincent Millay wrote the poem "God's World," which is reprinted on pages 54-55. It first appeared in *Renascence,* published by Harper & Bros. in 1917.

ABOUT THE AUTHOR

Colleen Anderson lives in Charleston, West Virginia. In addition to travel and feature writing, short stories, poems, and short essays for West Virginia Public Radio, she has produced two collections of original songs, *Fabulous Realities* and *Going Over Home*. This is her first book for children. For information about author visits to schools, libraries, or other venues, please contact: Colleen Anderson, P.O. Box 525, Charleston, WV 25322 or visit www.colleenanderson.com.